The Stillwater Secrets

Rene' Stanley

BOOKS BY RENE'

Cover Design by Rene' Stanley

ISBN: 979-8-9997823-2-8

Library of Congress Control Number: 9798999782328

bbr@renes-books.us

https://booksbyrene.com

1 edition 2025

CONTENTS

CHAPTER 1

— · —

THE SENTENCE

The rage had been a living thing inside me for days, coiling in my gut like a viper, its venom seeping into every thought. Eleven years. Eleven years since Mom walked out and slammed the door not just on our house, but on our lives. Today marked the anniversary, and the silence in our apartment was louder than any shouting match. Dad had gone to work with his jaw set so tight I thought it might crack, Chloe had retreated into the fortress of her textbooks, and Ben... Ben had actually asked this morning if today was a "special day" because I looked even angrier than usual. That just about did it for me.

I didn't plan it, not really. Not the way you plan a vacation or even a weekend. It was more like the viper finally striking. One minute I was walking past Northwood Community Center, the place Mom used to drag us to for "enrichment activities," her voice echoing in my head about finding our "creative sparks." The next, my fists were clenched, and a rock I didn't even remember picking up was sailing through the big front window, the one with the faded mural of smiling, ridiculously happy kids.

The shattering glass was like a shout in the quiet afternoon. It wasn't enough. I found another rock. Then another. Each crash was a small, satisfying punctuation mark to the scream trapped inside me. It wasn't until a siren wailed in the distance, growing closer, that the red haze in my vision started to clear, leaving behind the familiar, bitter taste of ash.

***

The courtroom was cold, not just in temperature, but in the way the polished wood gleamed under the harsh fluorescent lights, the way everyone's voices seemed to echo with an official, uncaring hollowness. I stood beside a court-appointed lawyer who smelled faintly of stale coffee and whose tired eyes told me he'd already lost this fight before it began.

Dad sat a few rows back. I didn't look at him, but I could feel his gaze boring into my back, heavy with a disappointment that was worse than any yelling. Chloe and Ben weren't there. Dad had spared them that, at least. Or maybe he just couldn't bear for them to see this. To see me.

"Liam Michael Carter," Judge Ramirez said, her voice devoid of any emotion as she read from the papers in front of her.

"For the act of vandalism committed against the North-wood Community Center, a property valued by this city... significant damages... a pattern of escalating truancy..."

She droned on, listing my failures like a grocery list. My lawyer had tried to explain. Difficult home situation. Anniversary of mother's abandonment. Deep-seated grief manifesting as anger. Blah, blah, blah. Excuses. I knew what I was. A screw-up. A lost cause, just like the faded sign on the community center door.

Finally, she looked up, her dark eyes pinning me. "Mr. Carter, you leave this court with very few options. Your actions were destructive, irresponsible, and indicative of a young man who is either unwilling or unable to function constructively within society."

My lawyer tensed beside me. Here it comes, I thought. Juvie. The end of the line.

"Given your age, and the... mitigating circumstances presented by your counsel, and perhaps against my better judgment," Judge Ramirez continued, her gaze unwavering, "I am willing to offer you one alternative to the eighteen months in juvenile detention that the prosecutor is recommending, and which, frankly, you deserve."

Eighteen months. The words hit me like a physical blow. A year and a half locked away. My breath hitched.

"Your maternal aunt, Sarah Miller, and her husband, Mark Miller, of Havenwood, Virginia, have been contacted. They have... surprisingly, and commendably, offered to take you into their home, under their strict supervision, for a period of no less than the summer. This would be coupled with mandatory community service, regular counseling as determined by their local services, and adherence to a strict behavioral contract. Any deviation, Mr. Carter, any at all, and the original sentence of eighteen months will be immediately enforced."

Havenwood? Aunt Sarah? I barely remembered her. Vague images of a kind smile and sad eyes at some family gathering years ago, before Mom... before. The idea of being shipped off to some strangers in the middle of nowhere, a "faith-filled country town" as my lawyer had reluctantly described it, felt like a different kind of prison.

"The choice is yours, Liam," Judge Ramirez said, her voice flat. "Eighteen months in the state's care, or a summer in Havenwood with family who, for reasons I may not fully comprehend, are willing to give you a chance you haven't earned. You have until I bang this gavel to decide."

My lawyer leaned in. "Liam," he whispered urgently, "take Havenwood. It's a lifeline."

A lifeline? It felt like being tossed from a sinking ship onto a slightly less leaky raft, still adrift in the same cold ocean. But eighteen months... I thought of Chloe's already worried face, of Ben asking why I was so angry. I couldn't do that to them, to Dad. The viper in my gut gave a final, defeated hiss.

My voice was hoarse, barely audible. "Havenwood."

Judge Ramirez's gavel came down with a sharp crack that sealed my fate.

***

The farewell at our apartment was a blur of awkward silences and things left unsaid. Dad's hand on my shoulder felt heavy, his eyes filled with a weary mix of pain and a desperate, fragile hope I knew I didn't deserve. "Just... try, Liam," he'd said, his voice rough. "For yourself. Try."

Chloe, ever the stoic one, just gave me a quick, stiff hug, her overachiever armor firmly in place. But I saw the glint of tears in her eyes before she turned away. Ben, bless his nine-year-old heart, just looked confused and sad. "Are you going on a long trip, Lee?" he asked, using my old childhood nickname.

"Yeah, Benny," I said, ruffling his hair, the gesture feeling foreign and clumsy. "Something like that."

Then I picked up the duffel bag that contained the sum of my current existence and walked out the door, leaving behind one kind of prison for another. Havenwood. Whatever awaited me there, I knew one thing: I was on my own. Always had been, always would be.

CHAPTER 2

— • —

WELCOME TO HAVENWOOD

The drive with Dad to the bus station had been suffo-
catingly silent. What was there to say? "Sorry I wrecked
your life along with mine?" "Don't worry, I'll be a model citizen in Nowheresville?" I'd opted for staring out the
window, the familiar cityscapes blurring into a gray smear
that matched my mood. The bus ride itself was even worse
– six hours of stale air, crying babies, and the endless,
monotonous drone of the highway, each mile taking me
further from everything I knew, miserable as it was.

When the bus finally hissed to a stop in what I presumed
was Havenwood – it was less a station and more a dusty
patch of gravel beside a gas station convenience store – a
wave of something cold and heavy settled in my stomach.
This was it. The start of my exile.

A woman with kind eyes, a slightly hesitant smile, and hair
the same sandy brown as my mom's used to be, stood
beside a beat-up but clean minivan. Aunt Sarah. She looked
older than the vague image I had in my head, lines etched
around her eyes and mouth that spoke of worry, or maybe
just life. A tall, solidly built man with a quiet, observant face

stood beside her – Uncle Mark, I guessed. He looked like he spent a lot of time outdoors; his skin was weathered, and his hands looked strong.

"Liam?" Aunt Sarah's voice was soft, a little uncertain.

I just nodded, hoisting my duffel bag onto my shoulder. It felt like it weighed a thousand pounds.

"It's good to see you, Liam," Uncle Mark said, his voice a low rumble. He didn't offer to shake my hand, which I was grateful for. I wasn't in the mood for forced pleasantries.

The drive to their house was filled with Aunt Sarah's attempts at light conversation – pointing out the "charming" town square (a couple of old buildings and a faded gazebo), the "lovely" scenery (trees, more trees, and the occasional cow), and asking about my trip (which I answered in monosyllables). I mostly stared out the window, taking in the picture-perfect houses with their neat lawns and flowerbeds. It was like stepping onto the set of some wholesome TV show from the fifties. It made my skin crawl. Each manicured hedge and freshly painted porch felt like an accusation, a stark contrast to the gritty reality I was used to. This place reeked of "nice," and I knew, deep down, that "nice" often hid its own brand of judgment.

Their house was a two-story colonial, white with green shutters, a wide front porch complete with a requisite porch swing. Of course. Inside, it smelled like cinnamon and something vaguely floral, a world away from the stale city air of our apartment. Two kids, a girl who looked a year or two younger than me and a boy who couldn't have been more than ten, materialized in the hallway, eyes wide with a mixture of curiosity and caution. My fan club, apparently.

"Liam, this is our daughter, Maya," Aunt Sarah said, gesturing to the girl. Maya had her mom's sandy hair but a more guarded expression. She gave me a small, polite, "Hi.""And this is Sam." The boy, Sam, was all freckles and nervous energy. He practically vibrated. "Are you really from the city?" he blurted out.

"Sam!" Aunt Sarah admonished gently.

"Yeah," I said, my voice flat. "Really."

Maya shot me a look I couldn't quite decipher – pity? Annoyance? She quickly looked away.

Aunt Sarah showed me to my room upstairs. It was small, clean, with a single bed, a desk, and a window overlooking the relentlessly green backyard. It felt like a guest room, a temporary holding cell. There was even a handmade quilt on the bed with little embroidered bluebirds. Bluebirds. Seriously.

After I'd dumped my bag, Aunt Sarah lingered by the door. "Liam," she began, her voice still soft but with an undercurrent of seriousness now. "We want you to feel... well, as comfortable as possible here. But there are some things we need to be clear about."

Here it comes, I thought. The warden's speech.

"Mark and I, we believe in second chances," she said, her gaze direct, meeting mine. "We wouldn't have offered to have you if we didn't. But this isn't a vacation. You're here because a judge ordered it, and there are expectations. Yours, and ours."

She ticked them off on her fingers. "Schoolwork, even though it's summer – we'll get you set up with some online courses to keep you on track. Chores around the house, same as Maya and Sam. Respect for everyone in this home, and that includes their belongings and their feelings. Curfew is ten on weeknights, eleven on weekends, unless it's a church night or a family activity. No secrets about where you are or who you're with." She paused. "And you'll be attending Sunday services with us. It's important to our family, and we think it's a good way for you to connect with the community in a positive way."

My jaw tightened at that last one, but I just nodded, keeping my face blank. Argue now, and it just proves their point.

"The community service Judge Ramirez mentioned," Aunt Sarah continued, "we'll get that sorted out in the next day or two. And counseling. There's a good family therapist in town, Dr. Evans—"

"Pastor Evans' wife, actually," Uncle Mark's voice rumbled from the doorway. He'd come up silently. "She's very well respected."

Great. The whole town was probably in on the "Save Liam Carter" project.

"We're not trying to make your life miserable, Liam," Aunt Sarah said, and her eyes held that same sadness I vaguely remembered. Maybe it was for my mom. Maybe it was for me. "We're trying to give you a safe place to sort things out, to make better choices. But it's a two-way street. We'll give you respect, support, and honesty. We expect the same in return." She took a breath. "Any questions?"

I shook my head. My only question was how fast I could get out of this wholesome nightmare, but I knew the answer to that one: not soon enough.

"Alright then," she said, a hint of relief in her voice. "Unpack. Settle in. Dinner's at six."

She left, closing the door softly behind her. I stared at the bluebirds on the quilt, a bitter laugh trapped in my throat. Welcome to Havenwood. My own private, sun-drenched, faith-filled prison.

CHAPTER 3

— · —

THE STILLWATER SECRETS

The first few days in Havenwood crawled by with the agonizing slowness of a slug climbing a sandpaper hill. I mostly kept to my room, the bluebirds on the quilt mocking my confinement. Meals were a tense affair, punctuated by Aunt Sarah's determinedly cheerful questions and my monosyllabic grunts. Maya, my cousin, regarded me with a kind of wary curiosity, like I was a strange species of poisonous frog. Sam, on the other hand, seemed to find me endlessly fascinating, peppering me with questions about the city, gangs (did I know any?), and whether I'd ever seen a dead body. Uncle Mark mostly just observed, his quiet presence a steady, unreadable weight in the background.

I helped with a few chores – mowing the impossibly large lawn, taking out the trash – doing just enough to keep Aunt Sarah from leveling "the look" at me, the one that said she was trying really hard to be patient. The online coursework she'd found was as dull as I'd expected, and I clicked through it with minimal engagement. My sketchbook became my only real refuge, its pages filling with dark, twisted versions of Havenwood's idyllic scenery – trees with grasping branches, houses with shadowed, empty windows.

By day four, Aunt Sarah's patience, gentle as it was, apparently reached its limit.

"Liam," she said after breakfast, as I was making my usual escape back to my room. "I've found a place for you to start your community service hours."

I stopped, my hand on the newel post. Here we go. Picking up trash along the highway? Scrubbing toilets at the town hall?

"The Havenwood Historical Society," she announced, a little too brightly. "Mrs. Albright, the curator, is a dear friend. She's a bit overwhelmed with preparations for the upcoming Founder's Day celebrations, and she could really use an extra pair of hands sorting through donations and archives."

My heart sank. The Historical Society. It sounded like a mausoleum of boredom. "You want me to sort old junk?"

"It's important work, Liam," she said, her smile not quite reaching her eyes. "Understanding a place's history can be very... enlightening. And Mrs. Albright is a remarkable woman. Besides," her voice firmed slightly, "it fulfills the terms of your agreement with Judge Ramirez. You start this morning. I'll drive you over."

There was no arguing. An hour later, I was standing in front of a stern, two-story brick building that looked like it hadn't seen a joyful moment since the Civil War. The bell above the door of the Havenwood Historical Society jangled with a sound that, to my ears, was eerily similar to the clang of prison bars. The air inside was thick with the smell of old paper, lemon polish, and something else... dust, ancient and undisturbed.

A woman with a tight grey bun, spectacles perched on the end of her nose, and a gaze as sharp as a freshly honed knife looked up from a large, leather-bound ledger. She had to be seventy if she was a day, but there was nothing frail about her.

"You must be Liam Carter," she stated, her voice crisp and devoid of any false warmth. It wasn't a question.

"Yeah," I mumbled, already hating this.

"Sarah Miller called. Said you were... available." The way she said "available" made it sound like I was a stray dog she was reluctantly taking in. "I am Elspeth Albright, curator of this society. Punctuality, I see, is a virtue you possess. Let's hope it's not your only one."

She rose, surprisingly agile, and gestured for me to follow. "We are currently cataloging acquisitions for the Founder's Day exhibit. Many of our older families have donated items over the years. Some are treasures, some are trivial. All of it needs to be assessed, cleaned, and recorded."

She led me to a back room, dimmer and even more crammed than the front. Boxes were stacked everywhere, overflowing with what looked like the contents of a hundred attics. "This," she said with a sweep of her hand, "is your domain for now. You will sort through these boxes. Create three piles: items of potential historical interest for display, items that are clearly rubbish, and an 'undetermined' pile. Nothing," she fixed me with that penetrating stare, "is to be discarded from the undetermined pile without my express approval. Is that clear?"

"Crystal," I said, my voice dripping with a sarcasm I hoped she'd miss. Or maybe I didn't.

She handed me a pair of thin cotton gloves. "And I expect focused work, young man. This isn't a place for daydreaming or," she glanced pointedly at the earbuds I hadn't even dared to put in yet, "distractions. The past demands respect."

For the next three hours, I was an inmate in a prison of forgotten memories. I opened dusty boxes filled with faded letters I couldn't be bothered to read, chipped china, tarnished silver teapots, moth-eaten baby clothes, and photographs of stern-faced people who all looked vaguely unhappy. The work was mind-numbingly tedious. My back ached. The dust made my nose itch. I sorted with a resentment that grew with every worthless artifact I handled, convinced this was just another elaborate form of punishment designed to break my spirit.

Mrs. Albright appeared occasionally, materializing silently like a specter to inspect my piles, her lips pursed. She'd pick up an item, murmur something unintelligible about its provenance or lack thereof, and then disappear again, leaving me alone with the ghosts of Havenwood's past.

This was going to be a very, very long summer.

CHAPTER 4

— · —

THE HIDDEN BOX

Days at the Historical Society blurred into a monotonous cycle of dust and decay. Mrs. Albright, or "Elspeth the Eternal," as I'd started calling her in my head, kept me supplied with an endless stream of boxes from Havenwood's deceased. I sorted, I cataloged in my sloppy handwriting on the forms she provided, and I resented every single minute. My only solace was the brief lunch break when I could escape to the small, overgrown patch of grass behind the building, eat the sandwich Aunt Sarah packed, and sketch the crumbling brickwork or the way the ivy seemed to be slowly strangling the life out of the place. It felt symbolic.

It was sometime during the second week of my sentence, deep into an afternoon that threatened to put me to sleep on my feet, that things took a turn. Mrs. Albright, after sniffing disdainfully at a box of what appeared to be someone's entire collection of porcelain cats, pointed a bony finger towards a dark corner of the archive room.

"That closet, Mr. Carter," she announced, "hasn't been properly inventoried since the Truman administration, or possibly earlier. It's likely filled with donations that were deemed too insignificant or too damaged at the time. See if there's anything salvageable. If not, we clear it out for more... promising acquisitions."

The closet was more of a deep alcove, shadowy and crammed floor to ceiling with items even more derelict than what I'd been dealing with. Cobwebs as thick as cotton candy draped everything. It smelled like damp wool and forgotten secrets. Perfect.

I started hauling things out: a stack of mildewed hymn books tied with rotting string, a headless dressmaker's dummy, a crate of chipped ceramic insulators, a truly hideous mounted deer head with one glass eye missing. Standard forgotten-closet fare. I was on autopilot, just wanting to get through it, my mind already drifting to how many hours were left until I could escape back to the relative freedom of Aunt Sarah's perfectly manicured lawn.

Then, tucked way in the back, behind a collapsed pile of what might have once been elaborate curtains, my hand hit something solid and wooden. I pulled it out, expecting another crate of broken pottery or rusty tools.

It was a box, but different from the others. Smaller, about the size of a shoebox, made of dark, unadorned wood, the lid slightly warped. There was no label, no dust – or at least, significantly less dust than everything else in that crypt of a closet, as if it had been placed there more carefully, or perhaps disturbed more recently than the Truman years. It felt... different. Heavier than it looked.

A flicker of something that wasn't boredom or resentment went through me. Curiosity? Not quite. More like a deviation from the expected, and right then, any deviation was welcome.

I glanced back towards the main room. Mrs. Albright was at her desk, her head bent over some ancient-looking tome. This was probably just more junk, another dead end in a day full of them. I should just add it to the rubbish pile.

But I didn't.

Instead, I carried it to a slightly cleaner spot on the floor, away from the direct line of sight from the doorway. The lid wasn't locked, just stuck. With a bit of effort, a reluctant creak, it opened.

Inside, nestled on a lining of faded, once-blue velvet, lay a strange little collection. A small, leather-bound journal, its cover worn smooth at the edges, a tarnished silver clasp holding it shut. A silver locket, intricately engraved but blackened with age, on a delicate, broken chain. And lying on top, a folded piece of parchment, yellowed and brittle, tied with a faded blue ribbon that looked like it would crumble if I breathed on it too hard.

This wasn't like the other stuff. This felt... personal. Deliberately hidden.

My fingers, still covered by the thin cotton gloves, reached for the parchment. Carefully, I untied the fragile ribbon. The parchment crackled as I unrolled it. Written in an elegant, spidery script, the ink faded but still legible, was not a letter, but a verse:

Where shadows lengthen, secrets sleep,

Beneath the gaze the elders keep.

The river whispers, the old stone sighs,

A truth concealed from prying eyes.

Seek the heart where memories dwell,

Lest history's echo bids farewell.

I read it once, then again. It was just a poem, probably some sentimental nonsense an old lady had written. But the words... they had a certain cadence, a feeling of hidden meaning. "Secrets sleep." "Truth concealed." My cynical brain wanted to dismiss it, but another part of me, the part that was suffocating in the blandness of Havenwood and the drudgery of my existence, snagged on it.

My first instinct, the one drilled into me by years of self-preservation, was to hide it. If this was anything re-motely interesting, Mrs. Albright would confiscate it, cata-log it, and stick it in a glass case with a boring little label. It would become another dead thing, another piece of Havenwood's dusty past.

But if I kept it...

It would be mine. A secret. Something that didn't belong to this town, or to my sentence, or to Aunt Sarah's well-mean-ing agenda.

The decision was instantaneous.

Quickly, before Mrs. Albright could materialize, I slipped the parchment and the locket into the deep side pocket of my hoodie. The journal was bulkier. I glanced around, then shoved it into the waistband of my jeans at the small of my back, the stiff leather pressing against my skin. My hoodie was loose enough; it wouldn't show. The empty wooden box, now just a container, I slid back into the deepest shadows of the closet, kicking some of the old curtain material over it. Out of sight, out of mind.

I took a deep breath, my heart thumping a little faster than usual. I grabbed a handful of the hymn books and the headless dummy, walked back into the main archive room, and dumped them onto the appropriate piles.

"Making progress, I see," Mrs. Albright commented without looking up.

"Yeah," I said, my voice carefully neutral. "Just a bunch of old junk, mostly."

She just grunted. But as I went back to the closet, a tiny, unfamiliar spark had ignited somewhere in the desolate landscape of my mind. It wasn't hope, not even close. But it was definitely something other than nothing.

CHAPTER 5

— · —

WHISPERS FROM THE PAST

The rest of that afternoon at the Historical Society was a strange mix of tedium and a new, thrumming undercurrent of anticipation. Every rustle of Mrs. Albright's papers, every creak of the old building, made me jump, convinced she somehow knew what I'd pocketed. The journal pressed uncomfortably against my back, a constant reminder of the secret I now carried. It was a relief when five o'clock finally rolled around and I could escape, the hidden items feeling like a forbidden weight in my hoodie and jeans.

Back in my bluebird-infested room at Aunt Sarah's, I waited until I heard the clatter of pans downstairs – Aunt Sarah starting dinner, Uncle Mark presumably home from work, Maya and Sam occupied. Only then did I dare to pull out my treasures.

I spread the parchment poem on the small desk first, smoothing out its creases. The spidery handwriting was elegant, a little shaky, like someone had poured a lot of emotion into those words. "Where shadows lengthen, secrets sleep... The river whispers, the old stone sighs..." It still sounded like something out of a bad fantasy novel, but now, holding it, knowing it was mine, it felt different. It felt like a map, even if I didn't know what it led to.

Next came the locket. It was heavier than it looked, tarnished almost black in places. I fumbled with the clasp, trying to find a way to open it, but it was stubbornly fused shut, probably by decades of neglect. Frustration pricked at me. What was inside that was so important it needed to be sealed away? I tried prying at it with a fingernail, then the edge of a coin from my pocket, but I was afraid of damaging it further. For now, it would have to keep its secret.

Finally, the journal. The leather cover was soft and worn, the silver clasp intricate but, thankfully, not locked. I opened it carefully, the pages stiff and yellowed, emitting a faint, dusty scent. The same elegant, spidery handwriting as the poem filled the pages, though in places it was hurried, almost frantic.

The first few entries were mundane – notes about weather, daily chores, mentions of "Father" and "Mother" with a kind of distant formality. Then, a name started to appear more frequently: Eleanora. It seemed to be the journal writer herself. I flipped through, scanning for anything that jumped out. There were descriptions of walks in the woods, clandestine meetings by an "old oak," and hushed conversations. A sense of secrecy, of something forbidden, began to permeate the entries.

"Met with H. today by the Stillwater bend," one entry read. "Father suspects, I know it. His eyes follow me everywhere.

But H. says we must be brave. Our friendship is worth any risk."

H? Who was H? The locket – did it hold a picture of H?

Another entry, a few pages later: "Eleanora, you are a fool for dreams, Mother says. But are dreams not the only truth worth holding when reality is so… constrained? H. understands. He alone."

There was a raw emotion in the words, a loneliness that resonated with a dull ache somewhere deep inside me. I, of all people, knew about loneliness, about feeling constrained by a reality you didn't choose.

I pulled out my sketchbook and a pencil. Usually, I drew what I saw, or the twisted versions of it that lived in my head. But now, I started sketching the words from the poem. I drew a winding river, trying to imagine what the "Stillwater bend" Eleanora mentioned might look like. I sketched a collection of old, weathered stones, one of them prominent, sighing in the wind. I drew the bird-like symbol I imagined might be hidden somewhere. The "gaze the elders keep" became a series of stern, shadowed faces, like the ones on old statues. My art, usually an expression of my anger or boredom, now had a new focus, a covert purpose. It was a way to think, to explore the clues without having to write them down literally. If anyone found my sketchbook, they'd just see my usual weird drawings.

Hours passed. The smell of roasting chicken eventually drifted up from downstairs, and Aunt Sarah called my name for dinner. I carefully hid Eleanora's journal, poem, and locket back under the loose floorboard, my mind still buzzing with questions.

Who was Eleanora? Who was H? And what secret were they so desperate to protect that it ended up in a hidden box, with a cryptic poem as its only guide?

For the first time since setting foot in Havenwood, I wasn't just counting the minutes until I could leave. I had a puzzle to solve. And for some reason I didn't quite understand, it felt important.

CHAPTER 6

—·—

THE OLD STONE'S SECRET

T he words from Eleanora's poem—"The river whispers, the old stone sighs"—had taken root in my mind, replaying like a half-forgotten song. For two days, I went through the motions: enduring Mrs. Albright's suspicious glares as I sorted through yet more of Havenwood's dusty detritus, picking at Aunt Sarah's meticulously prepared meals, and clicking aimlessly through online history lessons that felt about as relevant as the chipped teacups I was forced to handle. But beneath the surface of my carefully maintained indifference, the puzzle simmered.

I needed to get out, to see if these weren't just the ramblings of some long-dead girl. I needed to see if the "old stone" was a real place.

Saturday morning offered my first real chance. Uncle Mark was out on a carpentry job, Sam was at a friend's house, and Maya, after giving me a cursory glance that clearly labeled me as a social dead end, had retreated to her room with her phone. Aunt Sarah was in the kitchen, humming along to some soft Christian radio station while baking something that filled the house with the scent of apples and cinnamon. It was almost too wholesome to bear.

"Going out," I mumbled, grabbing my backpack with my sketchbook already inside.

Aunt Sarah turned, wiping floury hands on her apron. "Oh? Anywhere in particular, Liam?" Her smile was hopeful, like she expected me to announce I was joining the church youth group or volunteering to rescue kittens.

"Just... around," I said. "Gonna sketch." It was the perfect excuse. No one questioned an artist, even a delinquent one, if he said he was looking for inspiration.

She nodded, that little hopeful light dimming slightly but not extinguishing. "Alright, dear. Just be back for lunch, okay? Around one?"

"Sure."

I practically bolted out the door, needing to escape the cloying domesticity. I had a vague idea of where the Stillwater River was from Aunt Sarah's initial, awkward tour of the town – east side, near where the original settlement was supposed to have been. It wasn't much of a river, more like a wide, fast-moving creek, but it was the only named body of water that seemed to fit.

The quiet of Havenwood on a Saturday morning was different from the weekday quiet. It was less about emptiness and more about a slow, deliberate pace. People mowed lawns, kids rode bikes in lazy circles on the sidewalks, and the sun beat down with a lazy warmth. It still felt like a foreign country.

I found a dirt path that veered off the main road, marked by a battered sign that read "River Access – Unmaintained Trail." Perfect. Unmaintained meant fewer people. The path wound through thick trees, the air growing cooler and damp as I got closer to the water. The sound of the river, a constant, gentle rush, grew louder, and soon I could see glints of light reflecting off its surface through the leaves.

The bank was overgrown, a tangle of bushes and tall grass. I walked along its edge, my eyes scanning for anything that might resemble an "old stone" that "sighed." It felt ridiculous, like I was on some stupid treasure hunt from a kid's adventure book. But still, I looked.

After about twenty minutes of pushing through scratchy branches and swatting at mosquitoes, I was ready to give up. This was a waste of time. The poem was just a poem. Then, I saw it – not right on the bank, but set back a little, on a slight rise almost hidden by a curtain of willow branches. A jumble of large, moss-covered rocks. They looked ancient, like the tumbled-down ruins of something man-made a long, long time ago. One stone, flatter and broader than the others, sat slightly apart, overlooking a curve in the river. It was big enough to sit on, and the wind, funneled through the trees and across the water, seemed to make a low, mournful sound as it passed over it. Sighs, I thought, a small jolt going through me. This could be it.

My heart beat a little faster. I pushed through the willows, my sneakers sinking slightly into the soft earth. I sat on the flat stone, pulling out my sketchbook as a deliberate act of normalcy, just in case someone stumbled upon me. From here, I had a clear view of the river bending out of sight downstream. The air was cooler here, the sound of the water more distinct.

I ran my hand over the stone's surface. It was rough, pocked with age, covered in a thin layer of gritty moss in places. I looked around its base, kicking away a drift of dead leaves. Nothing obvious. No giant X marking the spot. Disappointment started to curdle the faint excitement. Maybe it was just a cool rock formation.

Then, my fingers brushed against something less natural. On the side of the large flat stone, the side facing the downstream curve of the river, almost completely obscured by a thorny, tenacious bush, was a carving.

I leaned closer, pulling the thorny branches carefully aside. It was faint, so weathered that it was almost invisible against the mottled grey of the rock, but it was definitely there. Not letters, but a symbol. A simple, incised outline that looked like a bird in flight, its wings swept back, its body a single, decisive line. Or maybe it was an arrow, sharply angled. Either way, it pointed distinctly downstream.

A shiver, completely unrelated to the cool air, traced its way down my spine. This wasn't just in my head. This was real. Someone had carved this here, deliberately. Eleanora? Or H?

My hand went to my pocket, to the folded parchment I now carried everywhere. "The river whispers, the old stone sighs..." And the old stone pointed a way.

I quickly flipped open my sketchbook, my earlier pretense forgotten. My pencil flew across the page, capturing the shape of the rocks, the curve of the river, and most importantly, the precise design and placement of the hidden symbol. My usual dark, brooding lines were replaced with something more urgent, more focused.

This wasn't just a random collection of words anymore. It was a trail. And I was standing at its beginning. The thought didn't bring a smile to my face – I wasn't there yet, not by a long shot. But it did bring a low thrum of something I hadn't felt in years. A reluctant intrigue. A sense that maybe, just maybe, there was something in this godforsaken town worth paying attention to.

And it was mine to figure out.

CHAPTER 7

— · —

CLOSE CALL

The discovery of the carved symbol by the river had lit a low, steady fire under me. For the first time, Eleanora's poem felt less like old words on brittle paper and more like a tangible map, a series of breadcrumbs leading somewhere real. The next few days at the Historical Society were still a grind, but now, amidst the dust and tedium, my mind was actively working, turning over the clues, trying to connect the symbol to the words, to Eleanora's half-whispered secrets in her journal.

Each evening, after the charade of family dinner where I pushed food around my plate and offered noncommittal grunts to Aunt Sarah's attempts at conversation, I'd retreat to my room – my bluebird-lined cell – and wait. The house had its own rhythm: the clatter of dishes being cleared, the low murmur of the television as Uncle Mark unwound, Maya's pop music drifting faintly from her room, Sam's occasional whoops or bangs as he played. I'd wait until those sounds settled into a more subdued evening hum before daring to retrieve my hidden treasures.

The loose floorboard under the bed had become Eleanora's new hiding place. It wasn't ideal, but it was the best I could come up with. Each night, I'd carefully pull out the journal, the locket, and the parchment.

Tonight, I was focused on the journal again, trying to decipher Eleanora's spidery script under the dim glow of the small desk lamp I'd angled to minimize light escaping under the door. The name "H." appeared frequently, always with a sense of hushed importance, sometimes with joy, other times with a thread of anxiety. "H. brought me wildflowers today, tucked them into the hollow of the old sentinel oak... Father would be furious if he knew I ventured so far alone, let alone met with H." Another entry: "The locket, H.'s gift, feels warm against my skin. A promise. A secret for only us to share."

So the locket was from H. I picked it up again, turning the tarnished silver over and over in my fingers, frustration mounting. It remained stubbornly sealed. What promise did it hold? What secret?

I was so absorbed, tracing the faded ink of one particularly emotional passage where Eleanora wrote of her fear of being "discovered and sent away," that I didn't register the almost imperceptible creak of a footstep in the hallway outside my room. My senses were usually sharper than that, honed by years of needing to anticipate trouble. But Havenwood, despite my best efforts to remain on guard, had a way of lulling you with its relentless quiet.

A soft knock on the door shattered my concentration. "Liam? Honey, you still awake?"

Aunt Sarah.

Panic, cold and absolute, seized me. My heart leaped into my throat. In a single, clumsy, adrenaline-fueled movement, I swept the journal, the locket, and the precious parchment off the desk, shoving them haphazardly under the pillow on my bed. I spun around in the chair, knocking my knee against the desk leg with a dull thud, just as the doorknob began to turn. I tried to arrange my face into something resembling casual boredom, hoping the sudden flush I could feel creeping up my neck wasn't too obvious.

Aunt Sarah opened the door a crack, her head poking in. Her expression was soft, framed by the warm light from the hallway. "Oh, goodness, did I startle you? Sorry to disturb you so late."

I swallowed, my throat dry. "No. S'fine. Just... thinking." Lame, so lame.

Her gaze drifted around the small room, lingering for a fraction of a second on the desk, then on the bed. Did she see the slight, unnatural lump of the journal under the pillow? Could she sense the frantic energy still crackling in the air? Or was that just my own guilty conscience screaming at me?

"I just wanted to see if you needed an extra blanket," she said, her eyes returning to mine, kind as always. "It's supposed to get a bit cooler tonight, and this room can be a little drafty."

"No. I'm good," I managed, my voice coming out a little too quick, a little too strained. I forced myself to unclench my fists, which were balled up tight at my sides.

Aunt Sarah lingered for what felt like an eternity, though it was probably only a few seconds. That gentle, slightly sad smile I was starting to recognize touched her lips. "Alright then," she said finally. "Try to get some sleep. You looked a bit worn out at dinner."

"Yeah. Will do."

She nodded and pulled the door mostly shut, leaving just a thin sliver of orange light cutting across the floor. I didn't move, didn't even breathe properly, until I heard the soft padding of her footsteps retreating down the stairs and the faint click of her own bedroom door closing.

Only then did I let out a ragged, shaky breath and slump back against my chair, my legs feeling like jelly. That had been way too close. My hands were clammy, and I could still feel the frantic thumping of my heart against my ribs.

I reached under the pillow and carefully retrieved the items. The journal felt warm, almost as if it had absorbed my panic. This whole secret investigation thing was getting more complicated, more dangerous than I'd anticipated – not dangerous in a back-alley city kind of way, but danger-ous to my carefully constructed walls, to my ability to just serve my time here unnoticed.

But the fear, the near discovery, didn't make me want to stop. If anything, it did the opposite. It solidified a stubborn, defiant resolve deep inside me. This was my secret, my puzzle. And I wasn't going to let them, or anyone, take it away from me.

I just had to be smarter. Much, much more careful.

CHAPTER 8

— · —

ELEANORA'S ECHOES

The near-discovery by Aunt Sarah had me on edge for days. Every time she looked at me a little too long, or asked a seemingly innocent question about how I was spending my time, I felt a jolt of paranoia. I became even more meticulous about hiding Eleanora's things, checking the loose floorboard twice before leaving my room and again before going to bed. My interactions at home, already minimal, became even more guarded.

At the Historical Society, I tried to act as bored and resentful as ever, hoping Mrs. Albright wouldn't notice the new, almost frantic energy buzzing beneath my surface. My main focus now, apart from the physical clues of the poem, was the name: Eleanora. Who was she? When did she live? What was her family name? The journal offered no last name, only intimate thoughts and that mysterious "H."

I started paying more attention to the exhibits I was supposed to be cleaning and ignoring. Glass cases displayed faded portraits of stern-faced men and women in old-fashioned clothes – Havenwood's founding families, their names displayed on small brass plaques. Peyton.

Blackwood. Harrison. Davies. No Eleanora. I scanned family trees meticulously hand-drawn on yellowed parchment, looking for her name tucked away on a forgotten branch. Nothing. It was like she was a ghost, leaving behind only a journal and a poem.

The locket remained my biggest frustration. I'd tried everything short of taking a hammer to it. The intricate silver was beautiful, even under the tarnish, but its secrets were locked tight. What was inside? A portrait of H? Another clue? The not knowing gnawed at me.

One morning, Mrs. Albright, after observing me listlessly dusting a display of ancient farming implements, surprised me. "Mr. Carter," she said, her sharp eyes narrowed, "I believe it's time you familiarized yourself more directly with Havenwood's prominent lineages. The Founder's Day exhibit will feature several displays on the families who shaped this town. I need you to go through the archived family Bibles in the records room. Cross-reference birth, death, and marriage records with the Peyton, Harrison, and Blackwood family files. We need to ensure our display information is accurate."

I stared at her. Was this a coincidence? Or did she suspect something? Her expression was, as usual, unreadable. The records room was a small, even dustier annex off the main archive, filled with heavy ledgers and metal filing cabinets. It was also blessedly private.

"Fine," I said, trying to sound put-upon. Inside, though, a different feeling stirred. This was an opportunity.

She handed me a key. "Treat these records with the utmost care. They are irreplaceable."

For the rest of the day, I was surrounded by the ghosts of Havenwood's most important families. I meticulously went through the heavy Bibles, their pages brittle and filled with elegant, looping script recording generations of joy and sorrow. I cross-referenced the names she'd given me, making notes on the forms provided. It was tedious, detailed work, but it was a world away from sorting broken china.

And all the while, I searched for Eleanora.

With access to these records, my search became more targeted. The journal entries mentioned events that felt like they belonged to the late 19th or early 20th century, based on the language and descriptions. I started focusing on families prominent during that period.

Hours passed. The only sounds were the rustle of ancient paper and the scratching of my pencil. Just as I was starting to think this too was a dead end, I found it. Tucked into the back of a Harrison family Bible, in a section listing distant cousins and relations who had moved away or married into less prominent lines, was a faint, spidery entry: Eleanora Mayhew Harrison. Born 1872. Departed this life 1890.

Eighteen. She had died at eighteen.

A strange coldness washed over me. Eleanora wasn't just some old lady writing sentimental poetry. She was a girl, barely older than me, whose life had been cut short. "A promise to be kept, even beyond the veil," she'd written in her journal. Was that what this was about? Something she couldn't finish?

Beneath her name, in even fainter ink, was a small, almost illegible notation: "Interred at Old Grace Churchyard."

Old Grace Churchyard. I knew that place. Or at least, I knew of it. Aunt Sarah had pointed out the crumbling stone walls of the original Grace Church ruins on our first awkward drive through town, mentioning it was one of the earliest settlement spots, now mostly overgrown and forgotten, replaced by the newer Havenwood Community Church downtown.

I quickly scribbled "Eleanora Mayhew Harrison" and "Old Grace Churchyard" onto a scrap of paper, my heart thumping. This was it. This was the next step. Mrs. Albright's assignment had, ironically, given me exactly what I needed.

When I handed my completed cross-referencing notes to Mrs. Albright at the end of the day, she merely nodded, her expression unchanging. "Adequate, Mr. Carter. You may continue with the Blackwood files tomorrow."

I just nodded back, but inside, Eleanora's echoes were growing louder. She had a name. She had a place. And soon, I hoped, I'd uncover more of her secrets.

CHAPTER 9

— · —

THE GAZE OF THE ELDERS

Eleanora Mayhew Harrison. Died at eighteen. Buried at Old Grace Churchyard. The information replayed in my head all the next day as I dutifully, and with feigned boredom, sorted through the Blackwood family files for Mrs. Albright. My mind, however, was far away, picturing a forgotten graveyard, crumbling stones, and the ghost of a girl who'd died too young.

The line from her poem echoed: "Beneath the gaze the elders keep."

I'd initially thought of the stern-faced founder portraits in the town hall, or maybe the imposing statues in the town square. But now, knowing Eleanora was buried at Old Grace, it clicked. Where better for the "elders" of Havenwood—its earliest, most prominent deceased citizens—to "keep gaze" than in the town's oldest consecrated ground? Their tombstones would be their monuments, their silent, watchful presence.

My chance to investigate came that Saturday. Another weekend morning, another flimsy excuse about needing to "sketch." Aunt Sarah seemed pleased I was showing an interest in something, even if my sketches were probably not what she envisioned for a "nice young man." If she only knew what I was really drawing, what I was really seeking.

Old Grace Churchyard wasn't hard to find, though it was clear few people bothered anymore. It lay about a mile out of the main town, down a narrow, potholed lane that quickly turned to dirt. A crumbling stone wall, green with moss and half-swallowed by ivy, marked its perimeter. The original iron gates were rusted open at a permanent, lop-sided angle, like a weary sigh. No manicured lawns here. This place was wild, overgrown, and profoundly silent, save for the whisper of wind through the tall, untamed grass and the distant caw of a crow. It felt less like a cemetery and more like a forgotten corner of the woods that just happened to have stones jutting from the earth.

Perfect for someone who didn't want to be disturbed.

I pushed through the gates, the crunch of gravel under my sneakers sounding unnaturally loud. Headstones, tilt-ed at crazy angles, some so weathered the inscriptions were illegible, dotted the landscape. Obelisks dedicated to forgotten Harrisons, Peytons, and Blackwoods stood like ancient, solemn sentinels – the "elders," no doubt. Their stony gaze seemed to follow me as I moved deeper into the yard.

My first task was to find Eleanora. It took a while. I had to push aside tangled vines and decipher moss-obscured carvings. Many of the older stones were simple, heart-breakingly small for children who hadn't made it. Then, in a slightly more secluded section, beneath the heavy branches of an ancient, gnarled oak – perhaps Eleanora's "sentinel oak" from the journal? – I found her.

ELEANORA MAYHEW HARRISON

Born August 12, 1872

Entered into Eternal Rest October 5, 1890

A Beloved Daughter. Thy Will Be Done.

Eighteen years, one month, and twenty-three days. I did the math in my head. A strange pang, something too close to sadness, went through me. She was real. Not just a name in a book, but someone who had lived and breathed and, apparently, kept secrets.

Her headstone was simpler than some of the more ostentatious monuments nearby. It was grey granite, relatively unadorned except for a small, delicately carved lily at the top – a symbol of purity, or maybe sorrow. I looked around. The "elders" were certainly keeping their gaze here. Towering tombstones of various Harrison patriarchs and matriarchs surrounded her plot, their inscriptions boasting of long lives and civic duties.

Okay, so Eleanora was here, under their gaze. Now what? Was there another symbol? Another clue?

I sat on the edge of a low, crumbling stone wall nearby, pulling out my sketchbook as cover. I sketched Eleanora's stone, the ancient oak, the way the shadows from the larger monuments fell across her simpler grave. As I drew, my eyes scanned every detail of her headstone and the ones immediately surrounding it. I was looking for anything out of place, anything that didn't fit the funereal conventions.

It was on the largest, most imposing monument – a tall, weathered obelisk dedicated to a Hezekiah Harrison, Esteemed Founder, Pillar of the Community, 1820-1888 – that I saw it. Hezekiah. Could this be Eleanora's "Father" from the journal, the one whose disapproval she feared? He died two years before she did.

The obelisk was covered in flowing script detailing Hezekiah's accomplishments. But it wasn't the words that caught my attention. It was a small, almost insignificant detail near the base, on the side facing Eleanora's grave. Tucked into a decorative flourish of carved ivy, almost invisible unless you were specifically looking for something, was a tiny, incised number: **3**.

Just the number three. Nothing else.

It was so small, so easy to miss. Was it a mason's mark? Vandalism? Or was it a deliberate clue, linked to Eleanora's poem? I thought back to the bird/arrow symbol I'd found on the stone by the river. That had been subtle too. This felt similar.

"Beneath the gaze the elders keep." The elders were here. And Hezekiah Harrison, one of the foremost elders, had a number three carved into his monument, facing Eleanora.

I quickly sketched the number, its placement, the ivy design around it. What did "3" mean? The third verse of the poem? The third turning of a path? The third something from somewhere?

A new layer of the puzzle had just clicked into place. The old stone by the river had pointed a direction. Now, the elders in the churchyard had given me a number. The trail was getting more complex, but also clearer.

A cold gust of wind rustled the leaves overhead, making the shadows dance across the graves. It was time to go. I'd been here long enough. But as I walked back through the rusted gates, leaving Eleanora and the elders to their silent watch, I felt a new sense of purpose. The secrets of Stillwater were slowly, reluctantly, beginning to yield.

CHAPTER 10

— · —

SUNDAY AWKWARDNESS

The small victory at Old Grace Churchyard, the discovery of the number three, simmered in the back of my mind all Saturday afternoon. It was a secret warmth, a private puzzle that made the endless green of Havenwood seem slightly less oppressive. But Sunday morning dawned with the familiar dread of forced compliance. Church.

Aunt Sarah didn't demand; she "invited." Her tone, as she asked if I'd join them, was light, almost casual, but there was an underlying expectation that was as solid as the oak newel post in their hallway. "Liam, we'd love for you to come with us to Havenwood Community this morning," she'd said at breakfast, her smile hopeful. "It's a big part of our lives here, and Pastor Evans is such a good man."

My internal response was a silent groan. Church was the last place I wanted to be. I mumbled something about having a lot of online coursework to catch up on.

"I understand it might not feel like your thing right now, Liam," she replied, her voice still gentle but with that familiar firmness creeping in. "But part of your agreement with Judge Ramirez was to engage with the community and positive influences. We see this as part of that. We're not asking you to believe anything you don't, just to come and be present with us, as part of the family."

The reminder of the judge, the subtle leverage, was enough. Arguing would just make it worse, make me look like the defiant delinquent they probably all thought I was anyway. "Fine," I bit out, trying to load the single word with as much resentment as possible. "But don't expect me to start singing or anything."

A flicker of something – hurt? Disappointment? – crossed Aunt Sarah's face before she quickly masked it. "That's alright, dear."

Havenwood Community Church was exactly what I expected: a neat brick building with a tall white steeple, a perfectly manicured lawn, and a parking lot rapidly filling with sensible sedans and minivans. Inside, the air smelled faintly of old hymnbooks and coffee. I felt like an alien under a microscope as we walked in, Aunt Sarah nodding and smiling at people who all seemed to know each other. I could feel their curious glances, the polite, quickly averted stares. No doubt the news of the "troubled nephew from the city" had made the rounds. I slouched into the polished wooden pew between Uncle Mark, whose quiet solidity was oddly grounding, and Sam, who immediately started fidgeting with the bulletin. Maya sat on Aunt Sarah's other side, looking serene and perfectly at home.

The service began. I stood when they stood, sat when they sat, my arms crossed tightly over my chest, a permanent scowl my only contribution. The hymns were saccharine, the prayers felt rehearsed, and the communal responses made my skin crawl with their practiced sincerity.

Then Pastor Evans stepped up to the pulpit. He was a man in his late fifties, kind-faced, with a warm, earnest voice – the type of man who probably genuinely believed all the stuff he was about to say. Today's sermon topic, he announced with a gentle smile, was the Parable of the Prodigal Son.

My internal alarm bells didn't just ring; they clanged. Seriously?

As he spoke about the younger son demanding his inheritance, leaving home, squandering his wealth in "wild living," and ending up broke and shamed in a pigsty, I felt my face grow hot. Every word felt like a perfectly aimed dart, each one hitting a raw nerve. He's talking about me. The recklessness, the bad choices, the disgrace – it was my story, gift-wrapped in biblical allegory for the whole town to hear. I was convinced Aunt Sarah had given him a full briefing on my pathetic life. "And then, dear Pastor, he vandalized a community center because he missed his mommy..."

When Pastor Evans transitioned to the father's unconditional forgiveness, the robe, the ring, the fatted calf, I nearly scoffed out loud. Easy for you to say, Pastor. Some fathers just ran out of patience. Some mothers never looked back. The concept of such an easy, welcoming return felt like a fairy tale, a cruel joke designed to highlight my own irreparable situation. The more he spoke of grace, redemption, and the celebration for the son who "was lost and now is found," the more I felt like a specimen pinned to a board, every flaw exposed. My jaw ached from clenching it so hard.

The service eventually ended. I was already halfway to the exit, desperate for escape, when Pastor Evans intercepted us near the doorway, Aunt Sarah beaming beside him.

"Pastor Evans, this is our nephew, Liam, who's staying with us," Aunt Sarah said, her voice full of warmth.

The pastor extended a hand, his smile wide and, I had to admit, genuinely friendly. "Liam, so good to have you with us this morning. Welcome to Havenwood Community."

I managed a stiff nod, briefly touching his hand. It felt like shaking hands with my jailer.

"Hope you felt something in the message today," he continued, his gaze earnest. "That story of the lost son, it speaks to all of us at different times in our lives, doesn't it? That journey back home can be a powerful one."

My stomach tightened. He definitely knows. "It was... a story," I mumbled, staring at a point somewhere past his left ear.

He didn't seem fazed by my award-winning enthusiasm. "Well, son," he said, giving my shoulder a well-meaning pat that made me want to shrug off my skin, "if you ever want to talk about... well, anything at all, my door is always open. We're all just trying to find our way, aren't we?"

I mumbled something incoherent and made my escape, practically bolting past the smiling, coffee-sipping congregants. Aunt Sarah looked a little crestfallen as she and Uncle Mark followed me out.

Back at the house, the afternoon stretched before me, long and suffocating. The church visit hadn't brought me any closer to understanding these people or their faith. It had just carved the lines of my isolation a little deeper, leaving me feeling raw, angry, and more convinced than ever that I didn't belong. And somehow, that pastor, with his kind eyes and knowing sermon, had made it all intensely, uncomfortably personal.

Chapter 11

—·—

Maya's Observation

The uncomfortable Sunday experience left me even more determined to keep my head down and my real activities – the Eleanora investigation – completely under wraps. I retreated further into myself at home, if that was even possible, and at the Historical Society, I feigned an almost catatonic level of boredom while secretly piecing together the clues from the poem and Eleanora's journal. The number "3" I'd found at Old Grace Churchyard – what did it signify? The third grave from a certain point? The third line of a verse I hadn't yet understood? The third something else entirely?

My sketching expeditions became more frequent. I had to revisit the old stone by the river, re-examine the symbol. I needed to spend more time in the churchyard, trying to understand the significance of that number three in relation to Eleanora's grave and the imposing Harrison obelisk. I told Aunt Sarah I was working on a "series" – studies of old architecture and nature – and she seemed to accept it, probably just relieved I was voluntarily leaving the house.

But my increased absences and focused intensity when I was sketching hadn't gone entirely unnoticed. Maya, my fifteen-year-old cousin, was more observant than I'd given her credit for. She had this way of watching people from under her lashes, quiet and thoughtful, a stark contrast to Sam's boisterous curiosity.

One afternoon, I was spread out on the living room floor, my sketchbook open, comparing my drawing of the symbol from the river stone with the number three from the obelisk, trying to see if there was any stylistic similarity, any visual connection. I was so engrossed I didn't hear Maya come in until she spoke.

"Whatcha drawing that's so intense?"

I jumped, slamming the sketchbook shut. My heart hammered. "Nothing," I snapped, probably too defensively. "Just... stuff."

Maya raised an eyebrow, a hint of amusement in her usually serious expression. "Looked like more than 'stuff.' You've been sketching a lot of really specific, kinda weird places lately. The old ruins by the river? The creepy part of the churchyard? Most people stick to the town square or the covered bridge."

I scrambled to gather my pencils, avoiding her gaze. "I like old things.Atmospheric."

"Huh," she said, unconvinced. She perched on the arm of the sofa, watching me. "You know, those places have stories. Legends, even. Especially Old Grace. People say it's haunted."

"I don't believe in ghosts," I muttered, shoving my sketch-book into my backpack.

"Me neither," she said easily. "But old places have old se-crets. Sometimes people go looking for them." Her eyes held mine for a beat too long, a knowing glint in them that made me deeply uncomfortable. Was she just making conversation, or was she fishing? Had she seen more than I realized?

"Well, I'm just looking for decent light and interesting textures," I said, trying to sound dismissive. "Guess your thrilling Havenwood legends are safe from me." I stood up, needing to create distance.

"Okay," she said with a small shrug, but her gaze still felt a little too sharp. I retreated to my room, rattled. Maya wasn't hostile, not like some of the kids I knew back in the city. But she was smart. I'd have to be even more careful if she was paying attention to my comings and goings.

Later that evening, Sam provided an unexpected, innocent diversion. He was sprawled on the floor beside me while I was trying to read – or pretend to read – a book Aunt Sarah had optimistically given me about a troubled teen finding redemption through faith and farm work (seriously). Sam was chattering about his day, a non-stop monologue that usually faded into background noise for me.

"...and Mrs. Gable, my Sunday School teacher?" he was saying, "She told us about the first church, Old Grace, and how the really, really old families all got buried there, even before the town was super big. And she said some of them had, like, special family crypts or something, but they got all sealed up a long, long time ago because... because of... I dunno, badgers?"

I almost snorted. Badgers. But then a phrase snagged my attention. "Special family crypts? Sealed up?"

Sam nodded enthusiastically. "Yeah! Like secret rooms underground! She said one of the really old pastors, maybe Pastor Blackwood from way back, wrote in a church diary about how he had to seal one up himself because it was... um... unsafe. Or maybe it was just full of treasure and he didn't want anyone to steal it for the pirates!"

My mind flashed to Eleanora's journal, her fear of her "Father," the intensity of her secret with "H." The Harrisons were one of those "really, really old families." Could her "truth concealed from prying eyes" be hidden in something like a sealed family crypt at Old Grace? And the number three... could it relate to a specific crypt, or a location within one?

"A church diary, huh?" I asked, trying to sound casual. "That sounds... old."

"Super old!" Sam confirmed. "Mrs. Gable said all the oldest church records, like from before they built the new church, are probably locked up super safe over at the Historical Society. Because they're like, super valuable."

My gaze drifted towards my backpack, where Eleanora's journal lay hidden. The Historical Society. Of course. Mrs. Albright, with her keys to every forgotten corner and dusty record in Havenwood.

Sam had already moved on, now explaining the intricate rules of a game he'd invented involving alien squirrels and laser-beam acorns. But his innocent chatter had just given me a new, critical piece to consider. Sealed crypts. Old church diaries. And the key to it all might just be languishing in the very place I was forced to spend my days.

Maya's observation had made me realize I wasn't as invisible as I thought. But Sam's accidental breadcrumb had just pointed my investigation in a much more specific, and potentially fruitful, direction.

CHAPTER 12

— · —

A CRACK IN THE FACADE

The idea of sealed crypts and old church diaries chewed at the edges of my mind for the next few days. It added a new layer of urgency, a new target for my research at the Historical Society, though I knew I couldn't just ask Mrs. Albright to see Pastor Blackwood's "secret treasure map diary." I'd have to be patient, observant, wait for another "coincidental" assignment or an opportunity to snoop.

But Havenwood, it turned out, had more than one way to throw me off balance. It wasn't all ancient secrets and suspicious cousins. There was still the raw, gaping wound of my life back in the city, a wound that throbbed with a steady, painful pulse.

It was a Tuesday evening. Dinner had been the usual exercise in strained politeness. I'd managed to escape to my room, ostensibly to work on my online courses, but really to pore over my sketches of the churchyard and the river stone, trying to make sense of the number three and the bird-arrow symbol. The locket still lay on my desk, a frustratingly silent silver enigma.

The house phone rang downstairs – a shrill, old-fashioned sound I still wasn't used to. A minute later, Aunt Sarah's voice called up the stairs. "Liam? It's your father."

My stomach instantly clenched. Dad usually called on Sundays, a brief, dutiful check-in that was more about obligation than actual conversation. A Tuesday call felt... wrong. Ominous.

I trudged downstairs to the kitchen, where the phone hung on the wall, its curly cord a relic from another era. Aunt Sarah was at the sink, her back to me, but I could tell she was listening. I grabbed the receiver. "Yeah?"

"Liam. It's Dad." His voice sounded tired, stretched thin, like an old rubber band about to snap.

"Hey," I said. "Everything okay?" Even as I asked, I knew it wasn't.

A long sigh crackled through the line. "Not really, son. It's... it's Chloe."

My breath caught. Chloe, my overachieving, always-in-control sister. What could be wrong with Chloe? "What happened? Is she sick?"

"Not sick, not exactly." Dad paused, and I could hear the exhaustion in that silence. "Her grades came out. She... she didn't do as well as she expected. As we expected. Straight A's have always been her thing, you know? But she got a B-plus in algebra and a B in history. And she's... well, she's taking it hard, Liam. Really hard. Locked herself in her room, won't talk to me. Says she's a failure."

A B-plus and a B. That was Chloe's crisis? Back in my world, that was practically honor roll. But for Chloe, whose entire sense of self seemed wrapped up in being perfect, I could almost understand. Almost. "It's not the end of the world, Dad," I said, trying for a reassuring tone that felt hollow even to me.

"I know that, you know that. But try telling her that." Another sigh, heavier this time. "She's been under a lot of stress, with... well, with everything. You being gone, me working extra shifts to cover... things. I think it's all just caught up with her." He didn't say "to cover the damages you caused," but it hung in the air between us, unspoken and heavy. "And Ben's been asking more questions about your mom again. He found an old photo album..."

Guilt, sharp and familiar, twisted in my gut. My stupid, impulsive act of vandalism hadn't just landed me in Havenwood; its ripples were still spreading, making things harder for the people I'd left behind. Chloe crumbling, Dad overwhelmed, Ben dredging up old pain. All because of me.

"I... I don't know what to say, Dad," I mumbled, feeling useless.

"There's nothing to say, really. I just... I thought you should know. Maybe you could try calling her later this week? Talk to her? She always used to listen to you, back before..." Before I became a walking disaster.

"Yeah. Okay. I'll try."

We hung up a few minutes later, the conversation ending with the usual strained affirmations. I stood there in Aunt

Sarah's cheerful yellow kitchen, the receiver still cold in my hand, feeling like the walls were closing in. The weight of it all – my mom's abandonment, my own screw-ups, Chloe's breakdown, Dad's quiet despair – suddenly felt crushing.

I didn't realize Aunt Sarah had turned from the sink until she was standing beside me, her expression full of a soft concern that made me want to recoil. "Everything alright, Liam?" she asked gently.

The carefully constructed facade I wore, the one that said I don't care, nothing touches me, began to crack. I could feel the sting of unexpected tears behind my eyes, a tightening in my throat. I blinked rapidly, turning away from her, angry at myself for this show of weakness.

"It's fine," I choked out, my voice rough. "Just... stuff back home."

I expected a lecture, a platitude, maybe even an "I told you so" disguised as concern. Instead, Aunt Sarah just placed a warm hand lightly on my arm. "Family troubles are heavy burdens to carry alone, Liam," she said, her voice incredibly soft. "You don't always have to be so strong, you know. It's okay to lean sometimes."

Her touch, her quiet words, were so unexpected, so different from the judgment or indifference I was used to, that it caught me off guard. For a split second, I actually did want to lean, to let some of the crushing weight fall away. The impulse was so strong it terrified me.

I pulled my arm away, shrugging off her hand, the movement jerky and defensive. "I'm fine," I repeated, more harshly this time. I couldn't look at her. I couldn't let her see the crack. "Just tired."

I turned and practically fled back to the sanctuary of my room, leaving her standing alone in the kitchen. I slammed the door, my breath coming in ragged gasps, and threw myself onto the bed, burying my face in the stupid bluebird quilt. The tears finally came then, hot and angry, not just for Chloe or Dad, but for myself, for the mess my life had become, for the aching loneliness that even a town full of "nice" people couldn't touch.

Aunt Sarah didn't follow me. She didn't press. But later, when I finally emerged, red-eyed and hollowed out, to get a glass of water, I found a small plate on the kitchen counter with two freshly baked cookies and a note in her neat handwriting: "Thinking of you. – Aunt Sarah."

I ate the cookies standing by the sink in the dark, the gesture a tiny, unexpected crumb of comfort in the vast emptiness I felt. It didn't fix anything. But it was... something. A crack in my own facade, maybe. A tiny, hesitant admission that not everyone was out to judge, or to leave.

CHAPTER 13

— · —

THE LOCKET OPENS

The emotional fallout from the phone call with Dad, and Aunt Sarah's quiet act of kindness, left me feeling unsettled for days. It was easier to be angry and resentful; those feelings were familiar, like a well-worn coat. Vulnerability, on the other hand, felt like walking around with no skin – everything was too raw, too exposed. I threw myself back into the Eleanora mystery with a renewed, almost desperate focus. It was a welcome distraction, a puzzle with defined edges, unlike the messy, unsolvable problems of my own life.

The locket was still my main obsession. I'd tried everything I could think of to open it – gentle prying with a pin, tapping it, even (in a moment of extreme frustration) briefly considering asking Uncle Mark if he had any delicate tools for his carpentry that might work, before dismissing the idea as too risky. It remained stubbornly sealed, its silver surface reflecting my own thwarted expression.

The breakthrough came unexpectedly, not through force, but through observation – a skill I was slowly, grudgingly, honing. I was at the Historical Society, enduring another lecture from Mrs. Albright about the proper way to handle fragile textiles (apparently, my technique with a box of nineteenth-century christening gowns was "barbaric"). To escape her critical gaze, I'd retreated to the records room under the guise of needing to double-check a Harrison family date.

While I was there, waiting for her to move on to tormenting some other aspect of my volunteer work, my fingers idly traced the engraved pattern on the locket, which I kept in my pocket. The design was intricate, a swirling pattern of what looked like ivy leaves. As I turned it over and over, I noticed a tiny, almost invisible seam hidden within one of the deepest curves of an engraved leaf, right near the hinge. It wasn't a clasp, not in the traditional sense. It looked more like a very subtle release mechanism.

My heart began to thump. Could it be that simple? That hidden?

Holding my breath, I pressed firmly on that tiny, disguised point with the edge of my thumbnail. For a second, nothing happened. Then, with a faint, almost inaudible click, the locket sprang open in my palm.

I nearly dropped it. My hands were actually trembling. After all this time, all this frustration, it had yielded.

I glanced towards the door of the records room, listening for any sign of Mrs. Albright. Silence. I was alone. Quickly, I cupped the open locket in my hands, shielding it from view.

Inside, nestled against the faded velvet, wasn't another cryptic message or a symbol. It was a miniature portrait, exquisitely painted on porcelain, no bigger than my thumbnail. It was of a young man.

He had dark, intense eyes that seemed to stare right through me, a serious set to his mouth, and a wave of dark hair that fell across his forehead. He was wearing clothes that looked to be from Eleanora's time – a high-collared shirt, a dark jacket. He wasn't smiling, but there was a certain romantic intensity to his gaze, a hint of a passionate, perhaps even reckless, spirit. He was handsome, in a brooding, old-fashioned sort of way.

This had to be "H."

Eleanora's secret love, the one she met in clandestine meetings, the one who understood her "foolish dreams." The one whose gift this locket was. Looking at his face, I felt a strange connection, a sense of intruding on something deeply private, intensely personal. This wasn't just about a hidden box and a cryptic poem anymore. This was about two real people, their forbidden love, their hidden promises.

And then, another thought struck me, colder and more unsettling. Eleanora Mayhew Harrison. She was from a prominent family. If her relationship with this "H." was so secret, so fraught with the fear of her "Father's" disapproval, it meant "H." was likely someone her family would not have accepted. Someone from a different social standing? Someone considered unsuitable?

The mystery suddenly felt heavier, more complex. This wasn't just a treasure hunt for a lost historical artifact.

This was about uncovering a potentially scandalous, deeply personal story, one that might have had serious consequences for Eleanora and H. The weight of their secret, carried for over a century in this tiny silver locket, settled onto my shoulders.

I carefully closed the locket, the click sounding unnaturally loud in the quiet room. My mind was racing. This changed things. Before, the mystery had been an intellectual puzzle, an escape. Now, it felt... realer. More human. And, in a way, more dangerous. Uncovering a forgotten love story was one thing; unearthing a potential scandal that might have caused Eleanora pain, or even contributed to her early death, was another thing entirely.

I suddenly felt a little overwhelmed, a little out of my depth. What had I stumbled into? And what was I supposed to do with it?

Mrs. Albright's voice, sharp and unexpected, cut through my thoughts from the outer room. "Mr. Carter, are you planning to take up permanent residence in there, or will you be gracing us with your assistance again today?"

I shoved the locket back into my pocket, my thoughts still whirling. The game had just changed. And I wasn't entirely sure I was ready for the new rules.

CHAPTER 14

— · —

WHISPERS AND WARNINGS

The face of the young man in the locket – H. – haunted me. His intense gaze seemed to follow me from the depths of my pocket. The mystery had shifted from an abstract puzzle to something deeply personal, centered around two young people whose lives and love had been shrouded in secrecy. My earlier, almost detached curiosity was morphing into something more complex, a sense of responsibility almost, to understand their story, to bring their hidden truth to light.

But with that came a new unease. If Eleanora and H. had gone to such lengths to hide their relationship, there had to be a reason. And unearthing that reason, over a century later, might not be a simple, harmless pursuit.

My focus at the Historical Society became twofold. I continued my assigned tasks for Mrs. Albright, meticulously cataloging the Blackwood family artifacts, but now my senses were on high alert. I listened more intently to her occasional pronouncements about Havenwood's history, hoping for any stray comment that might relate to Eleanora Harrison or her era. And I kept thinking about Sam's comment – the old church diaries, possibly held right here within these dusty walls. How could I get access to those without raising suspicion?

One afternoon, I was carefully cleaning a collection of antique surveying tools – compasses, chains, a beautifully crafted theodolite – all belonging to one of Havenwood's original town planners. Mrs. Albright was nearby, ostensibly supervising, though mostly she seemed to be ensuring I didn't drop anything irreplaceable.

"This town was built on strong foundations, Mr. Carter," she remarked, her voice startling me from my thoughts about Eleanora. "Surveyed with precision, planned with care by men of vision. Men like Hezekiah Harrison." She gestured to a stern portrait of him hanging on the far wall, the same man whose obelisk watched over Eleanora's grave.

"They understood the importance of order, of established lines," she continued, her gaze drifting from the portrait to me, sharp and penetrating. "They also understood that not everything from the past is meant for public consumption. Some things are... private. Family matters. Best left undisturbed, to maintain the integrity of what has been carefully built."

Her words were general, yet they landed with a peculiar weight. Was she just making a broad statement about historical preservation? Or was there a more pointed meaning? My hand instinctively went to my pocket, where the locket lay hidden. I felt a flush of heat creep up my neck.

"Some stories, Mr. Carter," she went on, her voice a low murmur, "are like old foundations. Dig too carelessly, and you risk unsettling the entire structure." She picked up a delicate porcelain doll from a nearby table, its painted smile fixed and unnervingly cheerful. "We preserve what is valuable, what edifies. We don't go looking for cracks simply for the sake of exposing them."

She then turned her attention back to the doll, tutting over a loose thread on its lace dress, as if the conversation had been nothing more than a passing thought. But her message, subtle as it was, had been delivered. Don't dig too carelessly.

It could have been a coincidence. She couldn't possibly know about Eleanora's journal, the poem, the locket. Could she? But the timing, her pointed gaze, the reference to Hezekiah Harrison... it felt like a warning. A polite, almost veiled threat, delivered with the gentle authority of someone who held all the keys to Havenwood's past.

That evening, the unease lingered. I was treading on sensitive ground. This wasn't just about finding a lost time capsule anymore. Eleanora's story, H.'s story, was tangled up with one of Havenwood's most prominent founding families. Uncovering it might not just "unsettle the structure," as Mrs. Albright had put it; it might bring down a whole load of unwanted attention on me – the delinquent from the city, already on thin ice.

The thrill of the chase was still there, but now it was accompanied by a new, chilling awareness. Some secrets, perhaps, were kept for a reason. And some people might prefer they stay that way. My investigation, which had felt like a private rebellion, a personal quest, suddenly seemed to have higher, more public stakes. And I wasn't sure I was prepared for the consequences if I kept pushing.

Chapter 15

The Heart Where Memories Dwell

M rs. Albright's veiled warning echoed in my thoughts for days, making me jumpy and even more secretive than usual. Every time she looked in my direction at the Historical Society, I half-expected her to ask what I'd been digging up, literally or figuratively. It made my covert research attempts feel riskier, laced with a new kind of paranoia. But her words, meant perhaps to deter, had an almost opposite effect. If Eleanora's story was sensitive enough to warrant such subtle discouragement, it only made me more convinced there was something significant to find.

I turned my attention to the next uncracked line in Eleanora's poem: "Seek the heart where memories dwell."

My first, most obvious thought was the Historical Society itself. Where else in Havenwood would more memories "dwell"? It was literally a repository of the town's collective past. For several afternoons, under the guise of my regular duties, I paid extra attention to the oldest sections of the archives, the displays detailing the town's earliest days. I looked for any mention of Eleanora Mayhew Harrison beyond the basic genealogical records I'd already found. I scanned old maps and photographs, hoping for some landmark or room designated as the "heart" of the original building or the early settlement. I found plenty of interesting historical tidbits – accounts of the first harsh winters, disputes over land boundaries, the triumphant arrival of the railroad – but nothing that felt like Eleanora's secret, nothing that resonated with the intensely personal tone of her journal.

My next guess was the town library. It was housed in another old building, though not as ancient as the Historical Society. Libraries were all about stories, memories preserved in books. I managed to spend an hour there one afternoon after my "shift" with Mrs. Albright, telling Aunt Sarah I needed to research something for my online coursework. I wandered through the quiet stacks, breathing in the familiar scent of old paper and binding glue. I even found a small local history section. There were a few slim volumes on Havenwood, mostly dry accounts of its founding and growth. I skimmed them, looking for any mention of Eleanora, H., or any unusual events around 1890. Again, nothing. Just facts and figures, no heart.

The number three, discovered on Hezekiah Harrison's obelisk, still nagged at me. Did it connect to this line? The third room in the Historical Society? The third shelf in the local history section? It all felt like grasping at straws.

I was sitting on my bed one evening, staring at my sketch of the poem, the locket with H.'s intense gaze lying beside it. The frustration was starting to build again. Maybe Mrs.

Albright was right. Maybe I was digging for something that wasn't there, or wasn't meant to be found.

Aunt Sarah's words from that night after Dad's call came back to me unexpectedly: "Family troubles are heavy burdens to carry alone..." And then, another memory: Eleanora's journal entry, "Eleanora, you are a fool for dreams, Mother says. But are dreams not the only truth worth holding when reality is so... constrained? H. understands. He alone."

Heart. Memories. Dreams.

Suddenly, the official, public places felt wrong. The Historical Society, the library – those were places of collective memory, civic memory. But Eleanora's secret was deeply personal, something hidden away from her family, from the town. Her "heart," the place where her most precious memories dwelled, wouldn't be a public archive. It would be something more intimate, something tied to her emotions, her secret life with H.

I thought of the locket, H.'s gift, which she'd written felt "warm against my skin. A promise." I thought of her clandestine meetings by the "sentinel oak," her fear of her father. Her memories weren't stored in ledgers or on library shelves. They were woven into the fabric of her hidden experiences, her feelings.

So, where would the "heart" of those personal memories be?

The old stone by the river, where I found the first symbol? It was a place of meeting, perhaps. Old Grace Churchyard, where she was buried? That was a place of finality, but also of remembrance. Her journal mentioned her room, her walks in the woods, the "sentinel oak."

The sentinel oak. The place H. tucked wildflowers for her. A place she went alone, or with him. A place of secret joy. Could an oak tree be a "heart where memories dwell?" It felt more plausible than a dusty archive, at least for Eleanora's kind of secrets.

And the number three... what if it wasn't a location marker in the public sense, but something more personal to her and H.? Three meetings? Three promises? Or maybe it related to a specific spot near that oak, or even the oak itself, if there were, say, three prominent trees together, or the third path leading to it.

A new line of thinking opened up. I wasn't looking for a building anymore. I was looking for a place that would have mattered deeply to a young girl in love, a girl trying to protect a fragile, forbidden happiness. The search had just become much more personal, and in a way, much more difficult. But it also felt like I was finally starting to think like Eleanora, instead of just a codebreaker.

CHAPTER 16

— · —

AN UNLIKELY ALLY?

The idea of the "sentinel oak" as the "heart where memories dwell" took hold. Eleanora's journal entries about it were some of the most vivid, filled with descriptions of wildflowers, whispered conversations with H., and the feeling of escape it offered from her "constrained" reality. If there was a physical place that held the essence of her secret life, that oak felt like it.

The problem was, Havenwood and its surrounding woods were full of oak trees. Old ones, young ones, entire groves of them. There was no "Sentinel Oak" marked on any town map I'd seen at the Historical Society. Eleanora's journal gave no specific directions, only poetic allusions to it being "deep within the whispering woods, where the sunlight dapples like golden coins."

For several afternoons, after my shifts with Mrs. Albright, I ventured into the wooded areas bordering the town, my sketchbook my alibi. I found plenty of impressive oaks, any one of which could have been a hundred years old or more. I sketched a few, trying to see if any particular tree or grouping matched the vague imagery from the journal, or if there was anything unusual about their surroundings. I looked for the number three again – three trees together, three branches pointing a certain way. Nothing jumped out. It was like looking for one specific leaf in an entire forest.

Frustration gnawed at me. I was so close to understanding this part of the poem, yet so far from pinpointing an actual location. The carved symbol by the river pointed downstream. The number three at the churchyard felt significant. But how did they connect to an oak tree that could be anywhere?

I was sitting on my bed one evening, staring at my growing collection of sketches – the river symbol, the number three, various ancient-looking oaks – feeling the familiar weight of a dead end pressing down. I couldn't ask Mrs. Albright; her earlier warning still echoed in my mind. Besides, asking her about a specific "sentinel oak" linked to Eleanora Harrison would be a dead giveaway. Uncle Mark knew the local area from his carpentry work, but how could I ask him without revealing too much?

My gaze fell on Maya.

Since our brief conversation where she'd noted my "weird" sketching locations, I'd been more aware of her quiet observations. She wasn't overtly friendly, but she wasn't hostile either. She was just... there. A normal teenager living a normal life in this too-normal town. She knew Havenwood. She'd grown up exploring its woods, its creeks, its forgotten corners in a way I never could in a few short months.

The thought of confiding in anyone, especially a member of the family I was forced to live with, made my stomach clench. Trust wasn't exactly my strong suit. Secrets were safer kept alone. But the image of H.'s intense gaze in the locket, Eleanora's faded, heartfelt words in the journal... they pushed at me. This wasn't just my secret anymore. It felt like theirs too, and I was just the unwilling custodian.

What if Maya knew of a specific, noteworthy old oak tree? Or a local legend about one? It was a long shot. And it meant sharing something. Risking ridicule, or worse, betrayal – what if she told Aunt Sarah everything?

I spent a restless night wrestling with it. By morning, I still hadn't decided, but the alternative – giving up, or blundering around the woods for weeks – felt worse.

At breakfast, Maya was, as usual, scrolling through her phone, a curtain of sandy hair hiding her expression. Sam was trying to balance a spoon on his nose. Aunt Sarah was bustling between the stove and the table. It was the picture of domestic normality that usually set my teeth on edge.

"Maya," I began, my voice coming out rougher than I intended.

She looked up, surprised. I rarely initiated conversation. "Yeah?"

"You know those... old places you mentioned? The ones with legends?" I fumbled, feeling like an idiot. "Is there, like, any really famous old tree around here? An oak, maybe? One that people might... you know... talk about?"

She frowned slightly, lowering her phone. "A specific old tree? Why?"

"Just... curious," I mumbled, feeling my cheeks warm. "For sketching. Looking for something with... character." Lame. So lame.

"There are tons of old oaks," she said, her eyes narrowed slightly, that observant glint back. "The woods behind Miller's Pond are full of them. Why that specific kind of tree?"

This was it. I could back out, mumble something, and retreat. Or I could take a tiny, stupid risk.

I took a breath. "Okay, look," I said, lowering my voice, even though Aunt Sarah was at the sink with the water running. "This is going to sound weird. But I found this... old poem. It mentions a 'sentinel oak.' And I think it might be a clue to something. Something historical. Not, like, treasure," I added quickly, seeing her eyebrow arch. "Just... an old story."

I didn't mention Eleanora, or the journal, or the locket. Just the poem and the oak. A small, controlled piece of the mystery.

Maya stared at me for a long moment. I braced myself for the scoff, the laugh, the "you're crazy" comment.

Instead, she tilted her head. "A sentinel oak?" she repeated slowly. "You know... there's this one really massive oak tree, way back in the North Woods, off the old logging trail. People don't go there much anymore. My grandpa used to say it was the oldest tree in the county, like it watched over the whole forest. He called it the 'Guardian Oak,' but 'sentinel' sounds kinda similar, right?"

My heart gave a small jump. "Guardian Oak? Where is it, exactly?"

"It's pretty deep in," she said. "Hard to find if you don't know the way. Why is this poem so important?"

I hesitated. "It's... complicated. But this tree, it could be a big piece of it."

Maya looked at me, then at her phone, then back at me. I could see the curiosity warring with her natural teenage skepticism. "So, you want me to... what? Help you find a tree because of some cryptic poem you found?"

"Maybe," I said, trying to sound casual, like her answer didn't matter, even though it suddenly mattered a lot. "You know the area. I don't."

She was silent for another long moment. I could feel Aunt Sarah's attention, even with her back turned. This was either going to be a breakthrough or a really embarrassing misstep.

"Okay," Maya said finally, a small, almost reluctant smile playing on her lips. "This Saturday. If you're not busy being a delinquent sketch artist, I'll take you to the Guardian Oak. But," she added, her expression turning serious, "if this involves anything actually illegal or gets me grounded, I'm blaming you entirely."

A wave of relief, so potent it almost buckled my knees, washed over me. "Deal," I said, maybe a little too quickly. "Thanks, Maya."

"Yeah, well," she shrugged, picking up her phone again, but I thought I saw a flicker of something new in her eyes – not just curiosity, but maybe, just maybe, a hint of interest. "Don't make me regret this, city boy."

I wouldn't. I hoped. I had an ally. An unlikely, possibly temporary, and almost certainly still suspicious ally. But it was a start.

CHAPTER 17

— · —

THE PRICE OF TRUTH

That Saturday morning, a nervous energy thrummed beneath my usual layer of practiced indifference. Maya was waiting for me on the porch, backpack slung over her shoulder, a determined set to her jaw that reminded me a little of Aunt Sarah. She didn't say much, just nodded towards the street. "It's a bit of a hike. Hope you wore decent shoes."

I had. My beat-up sneakers were probably the most practical thing I owned.

The North Woods were denser, wilder than the patches of trees I'd explored closer to town. Maya moved through them with an easy confidence, pointing out landmarks I never would have noticed – a strangely shaped rock, a particular bend in a nearly invisible stream. I followed, my sketchbook under my arm, acutely aware that I was trusting her, relying on her. It was an unfamiliar, unsettling feeling.

"So, this poem," she said, not looking back, "what makes you so sure it's about a real place?"

"Just a hunch," I said. "The details feel... specific." I still wasn't ready to tell her about Eleanora's journal or the locket. One step at a time.

After nearly an hour of walking, the trees thinned slightly, and we entered a sun-dappled clearing. In its center stood an oak tree so massive it made all the others look like saplings. Its trunk was gnarled and thick, its branches spreading wide like ancient, welcoming arms. It was, without a doubt, a sentinel, a guardian.

"Wow," I breathed, genuinely impressed. "That's... big."

"Told you," Maya said, a hint of pride in her voice. "This is the Guardian Oak. Or your 'sentinel oak,' maybe."

We approached it cautiously. The air around it felt different, stiller, older. I immediately started scanning its base, its lower branches, looking for any carving, any mark, anything that resembled the number three or the bird-arrow symbol.

"So, what are we looking for?" Maya asked, her skepticism returning slightly. "A big X? Buried treasure?"

"I don't know," I admitted. "A sign. A number. Anything that doesn't look natural." I thought of the "3" on Hezekiah Harrison's obelisk. Was there a connection?

We circled the tree slowly. Its bark was deeply furrowed, offering a thousand hiding places for a small carving. Then Maya, who was examining the tangle of exposed roots on one side, called out. "Liam, look at this."

Tucked into a hollow formed by three massive, intertwined roots snaking from the base of the oak, almost completely obscured by moss and dead leaves, was a flat, weathered stone. It wasn't a headstone, not like in the churchyard. It was smaller, rougher, almost like a stepping stone, but it felt deliberately placed.

My heart hammered. I knelt down, carefully clearing away the debris. And there, carved deeply into its surface, was the number **3**.

The same style, the same size as the one on Hezekiah's monument.

"No way," Maya whispered, her eyes wide. "That's... that's it? The number three?"

"It has to be," I said, a thrill shooting through me. "The poem, the grave, now this. It all connects." But what did it mean? Three roots? The third stone?

I ran my fingers over the number, then over the stone itself. It seemed firmly embedded in the earth. "Is this just a marker, or is there something under it?"

"You're not thinking of digging, are you?" Maya asked, her voice suddenly wary. "This looks really old. And we're pretty far out here. What if it's, like, sacred Native American ground or something?"

"Eleanora was from the late 1800s," I said, thinking aloud. "This feels... of her time." I pressed down on the stone. It didn't budge. I tried to wiggle it. Nothing.

"Maybe it's not about under it," Maya mused, tapping her chin. "Maybe it's about what you see from here, from the '3'." She stood up, positioning herself directly over the stone and looking out into the woods. "What direction does it point? Or what's the third significant thing you see from this spot?"

I stood beside her, following her gaze. The woods stretched out, a confusing tapestry of trees and shadows. Nothing immediately screamed "clue."

It was then that we heard it – a sharp crack of a twig breaking nearby, followed by a low cough.

We both froze. We weren't alone.

Maya grabbed my arm, her eyes wide with alarm. "Someone's here," she mouthed.

We ducked down behind the massive trunk of the Guardian Oak, hearts pounding. Peering through the leaves, we saw a figure emerge from the trees about fifty yards away – an older man, dressed in hunting gear, a rifle slung over his shoulder. He wasn't looking in our direction, just slowly making his way along what might have been an old game trail.

"Old Man Hemlock," Maya breathed, her voice barely audible. "He owns a lot of the land around here. And he really doesn't like trespassers. Especially kids."

Hemlock paused, looking around, sniffing the air like a hound. For a terrifying moment, I thought he'd seen us. But then he shrugged and continued on his way, disappearing back into the trees.

We waited, not daring to move, until long after he was gone. The silence of the woods felt different now, charged with a new tension.

"That was too close," Maya said finally, letting out a shaky breath. "If he'd caught us messing around here, especially if he thought we were digging..."

The thrill of the discovery was now tinged with a very real sense of risk. Mrs. Albright's warning about digging too carelessly suddenly felt much more immediate. We weren't just dealing with old poems and faded journals anymore. There were present-day consequences.

We didn't find anything else at the Guardian Oak that day. The encounter with Old Man Hemlock had spooked us both. As we hiked back to town, the conversation was more subdued. The "3" was a solid clue, but what it pointed to remained elusive, and now the act of searching felt heavier.

The weight increased that evening. Aunt Sarah got a call. When she hung up, her expression was serious.

"Liam," she said, finding me in the living room. "That was your probation officer, Mr. Henderson. He's scheduling a check-in call with you, me, and your father for next week. He wants a progress report."

My stomach dropped. A progress report. Just as things were getting complicated, just as I was treading on potentially dangerous ground with Eleanora's secrets, the system was reeling me back in, demanding I prove I was being a "good boy."

The pressure suddenly felt immense. Continue pursuing Eleanora's truth, with its unknown risks and the disapproval of people like Mrs. Albright and possibly trigger-happy landowners like Hemlock? Or retreat, focus on pleasing Mr. Henderson, on getting through my sentence without making waves, and let Eleanora's secrets stay buried?

The price of truth, I was beginning to realize, might be higher than I was willing to pay.

CHAPTER 18

— · —

DARK NIGHT OF THE SOUL

The looming check-in call with Mr. Henderson, my probation officer, hung over me like a gathering storm cloud. Every interaction with Aunt Sarah, every question about how my "community service" was going, felt loaded with an unspoken pressure to perform, to demonstrate that I was somehow being rehabilitated by Havenwood's wholesome air and dusty artifacts. It made the Eleanora investigation feel even more illicit, a reckless indulgence I couldn't afford.

Maya, to her credit, didn't push. After our encounter with Old Man Hemlock, she was noticeably more cautious. "Maybe we should lay off the creepy woods stuff for a bit?" she'd suggested, and I hadn't argued. The number "3" at the Guardian Oak was a solid clue, but what it signified remained a frustrating blank. Did it mean three paces in a certain direction? The third tree of a certain type? The third something mentioned in Eleanora's journal that I'd overlooked? I spent hours poring over my sketches and the journal pages, but nothing clicked. The trail had gone cold, and the weight of Henderson's impending judgment made it hard to focus.

The call itself was as awful as I'd anticipated. Dad was on the line, his voice carefully neutral. Aunt Sarah sat beside me at the kitchen table, her hands clasped tightly in her lap. Mr. Henderson's voice was professional, detached, as he went through his checklist. Yes, I was attending my volunteer hours. Yes, I was doing my online coursework. Yes, I was adhering to curfew.

But then came the kicker. "Liam," Mr. Henderson said, his tone shifting slightly, "while your aunt reports general compliance, I'm not seeing much in the way of... proactive engagement. Or demonstrable remorse for your prior actions. The reports from your city school before the incident were concerning, and the court is looking for a significant turnaround, not just ticking boxes."

My stomach clenched. "I'm doing what I'm supposed to," I muttered, my voice tight.

"Doing the bare minimum isn't always enough, Liam," he replied. "Judge Ramirez was clear: this was a chance to demonstrate real change. Frankly, from where I sit, it looks like you're just serving time. We'll need to see a more marked improvement in attitude and initiative if we're to recommend anything other than a return to more... structured supervision at the end of this placement."

The threat was clear. Juvie. The word hung in the air, unspoken but suffocating.

After the call ended, a heavy silence filled the kitchen. Dad had sounded disappointed, Aunt Sarah looked worried, her earlier optimism visibly deflated. I felt a familiar, bitter anger rise up. What did they want from me? Miracles? Did they expect me to suddenly transform into some well-adjusted, hymn-singing model citizen just because I was surrounded by trees and "nice" people?

"Liam," Aunt Sarah began softly, but I couldn't bear to hear it.

"Just leave me alone," I snapped, shoving back my chair and storming out of the kitchen, out of the house. I ignored her calling my name.

I ended up by the Stillwater River, not far from the spot where I'd found the first carved symbol. The water rushed by, oblivious. I picked up a rock, then another, the urge to throw them, to smash something, almost overwhelming. But the image of Judge Ramirez's stern face, Henderson's coolly disapproving voice, stopped me. That kind of release only led to more trouble.

The Eleanora mystery, which had briefly felt like an escape, a purpose, now seemed like a stupid, childish distraction. What was I even doing? Chasing ghosts? Trying to solve a century-old puzzle while my own life was crumbling? I was a failure. A failure at being a son, a brother, a "reformed youth." Even a failure at being a detective, apparently. The clues led nowhere. The number three was meaningless. The locket held a picture of a dead guy. So what?

Maya found me there an hour later, just as the sun was starting to dip below the trees, painting the sky in angry reds and oranges. She didn't say anything at first, just sat down on the riverbank a few feet away.

"Rough call?" she asked finally.

I just grunted.

"Look, Liam," she said, her voice surprisingly gentle. "I know things are... complicated for you. And maybe this whole Eleanora thing is just a distraction, like you said. Maybe it's nothing."

Her words, meant perhaps to be comforting, felt like another nail in the coffin of my already bleak mood. "Yeah, well, you're probably right," I said, my voice flat. "It's all just a stupid waste of time. Just like me being here."

I expected her to argue, to defend our discoveries. But she just sighed. "My mom tries really hard, you know," she said quietly. "She really believes people can change. She really wants to help you."

"Help me?" I scoffed, a harsh, ugly sound. "Nobody can help me. Can't you see that? I'm a lost cause. My own mother figured that out years ago. Took everyone else a while longer to catch on." The words were out before I could stop them, bitter and raw.

Maya flinched, and I saw a flicker of hurt in her eyes. Good. Maybe now she'd leave me alone too.

I stood up abruptly. "Forget the poem, forget the tree, forget all of it," I said, my voice hard. "I'm done. I just need to get through this summer, tick Henderson's stupid boxes, and get out of this godforsaken town."

I turned and walked away, leaving her sitting by the river, the unsolved secrets of Eleanora Harrison feeling as distant and irrelevant as the stars beginning to prick the darkening sky. The anger was back, a cold, familiar weight. But underneath it, for the first time since I'd arrived in Havenwood, there was a profound, crushing sense of hopelessness. I had no map for my own life, and chasing Eleanora's wasn't going to change that.

It was time to give up.

CHAPTER 19

— · —

A GLIMMER OF GRACE

I avoided everyone after my outburst by the river. I skipped dinner, ignoring Aunt Sarah's soft knock on my bedroom door. I lay on my bed, staring at the ceiling, the weight of Mr. Henderson's disapproval and my own self-loathing a suffocating blanket. Giving up felt like the only sensible option, a bitter pill of acceptance. Eleanora and her secrets could stay buried. I had enough ghosts of my own.

Later that night, long after the house had fallen silent, I crept downstairs for a glass of water, hoping to avoid any human contact. But as I passed the living room, I saw a soft lamplight spilling from under the door. Aunt Sarah was in there, curled up on the sofa, not reading or watching TV, just... sitting.

She looked up as I hesitated in the doorway. I expected disappointment in her eyes, maybe even anger after I'd snapped at her and Maya. Instead, her expression was just... tired, and filled with a sadness that seemed to echo my own.

"Couldn't sleep?" she asked quietly.

I just shook my head, ready to retreat.

"Liam, wait," she said, her voice gentle. "Please."

Reluctantly, I hovered by the door.

"What you said earlier," she began, her gaze steady on mine, "about your mother... about feeling like a lost cause... I know I can't truly understand what that's like for you. What either of those things feel like." She paused, and for a moment, I saw a flicker of deep, old pain in her own eyes, a reflection of the sister she'd lost in her own way. "But I do know that no one, absolutely no one, is beyond hope. Or beyond God's love, even when it feels impossibly far away."

I stiffened, ready for the sermon. Here it comes.

But it didn't. Instead, she said, "When my sister... when your mother left, a part of me broke. I was angry at her, angry at God, angry at the world. For a long time, I felt like there was this... gaping void where my faith used to be. I questioned everything. It all felt like empty words, hollow promises."

I stared at her, surprised into silence. Aunt Sarah, with her unwavering church attendance and her calm, steady faith – I'd never imagined her doubting anything.

"It wasn't a lightning bolt moment that brought it back," she continued, her voice barely above a whisper. "It was... slower. Quieter. Small things. The kindness of a friend. The unwavering support of Mark. Finding a verse in the Bible that suddenly made sense when it never had before. Little glimmers. Eventually, I realized that faith wasn't about having all the answers, or about life being easy and fair.

It was about choosing to believe there's something bigger than the pain, something good to hold onto, even when you can't see it clearly."

She looked directly at me, her eyes earnest. "I know you're hurting, Liam. And I know you feel like you have to carry it all yourself. But you don't. You're not a lost cause. Not to me, not to Mark, and certainly not to God. We just... we want to help you find a path through it, even if it's just by being here, by not giving up on you."

Her words, so unexpected, so devoid of judgment or platitudes, chipped away at the icy wall around my heart. She wasn't trying to fix me, not in that moment. She was just... seeing me. Seeing the pain I tried so hard to hide.

I didn't know what to say. "Thank you" felt inadequate. "I'm sorry" for snapping felt hollow. So I just stood there, a lump forming in my throat.

Aunt Sarah offered a small, weary smile. "There are cookies in the jar if you want one," she said softly. "Sometimes a cookie helps." Then she turned back to her quiet vigil on the sofa.

I got my water, and yes, I took a cookie. As I walked back upstairs, her words replayed in my mind. Little glimmers.

Back in my room, I didn't immediately fall into a pit of despair. Instead, almost against my will, I found myself pulling out Eleanora's journal and the sketches of the clues. I wasn't expecting anything. I'd told myself I was done. But Aunt Sarah's unexpected grace had stirred something, a tiny shift in the oppressive darkness.

I stared at my sketch of the number three from Hezekiah Harrison's obelisk, and the identical "3" from the stone at the Guardian Oak. What if it wasn't just a random number? What if it was more specific, more instructional?

My eyes fell upon Eleanora's poem, spread out on my desk.

Where shadows lengthen, secrets sleep,

Beneath the gaze the elders keep.

The river whispers, the old stone sighs,

A truth concealed from prying eyes.

Seek the heart where memories dwell,

Lest history's echo bids farewell.

I'd been focusing on the meaning of each line as a location. The old stone by the river. The elders in the churchyard. The sentinel oak as the heart.

But what if the "3" wasn't about a quantity, but a position?

The third line of the poem was "The river whispers, the old stone sighs." That's where I found the first symbol, the bird-arrow.

What was the third word of that line? River.

The third verse? There wasn't really a third verse, it was one continuous poem.

What if it was simpler? The number three. Three key locations.

1. The Old Stone by the River (with the bird/arrow symbol).

2. Old Grace Churchyard (specifically Hezekiah Harrison's obelisk, near Eleanora's grave, with the number "3").

3. The Guardian Oak (with the stone marked "3").

Three points. On a map, three points can define a triangle, or a specific area, or even a line if you connect them in a certain order.

My hand trembled slightly as I grabbed a blank page in my sketchbook. I drew a rough map of Havenwood as I knew it, marking the approximate locations of the river, the old churchyard, and the North Woods where the Guardian Oak stood. I placed dots for the three clue sites.

The Old Stone pointed downstream. The "3" at the churchyard... was it just a number, or did its position on the obelisk, facing Eleanora, mean something about direction from her grave towards the obelisk? And the "3" at the Guardian Oak – what did it signify there, other than confirming a link?

A previously overlooked detail from Eleanora's journal surfaced in my memory. An entry where she talked about H. showing her how to use a compass, how to find true north even in the deepest woods, calling it "our secret wayfinding." And another, where she mentioned pacing out distances for a "game" they played, a game of hiding and seeking messages.

Pacing. Directions. Three points.

A new thought, a tiny, hesitant spark, flickered to life. What if the clues weren't just individual locations, but parts of a larger set of directions? What if the number three, found at two of those locations, was a key to unlocking how they connected, or what to do next from one of those points?

It wasn't a solution. It wasn't even a clear path. But it was... a glimmer. A reason to look again, not with despair, but with a fresh, albeit fragile, sense of curiosity. Maybe, just maybe, I wasn't completely lost after all.

CHAPTER 20

— · —

THE FINAL SEARCH

A unt Sarah's words, and the unexpected shift in my own thinking about the clues, didn't magically fix everything. The dread of Mr. Henderson's disapproval still lingered, and the weight of my family's unspoken disappointments was a constant ache. But the oppressive hopelessness had lifted, just enough for a sliver of determination to break through. Eleanora's story wasn't over, and neither, I realized with a reluctant stubbornness, was my attempt to uncover it.

The first person I had to talk to was Maya. After my outburst by the river, I wasn't sure she'd even be willing to listen, let alone help again. But when I found her later that Sunday, ostensibly doing homework at the kitchen table, and quietly asked if we could talk, she just looked up, her expression neutral, and nodded.

We ended up on the back porch steps, the afternoon sun filtering through the leaves. I laid out my rough map of Havenwood with the three clue sites marked – the River Stone, Hezekiah's Obelisk at Old Grace, the Guardian Oak.

"Okay," I began, trying to keep my voice even, "I know I said I was done with this. But I was looking at it again... and I think the number three isn't just a random marker. I think it's about how these places connect. Like, actual directions, or pacing, like Eleanora mentioned in her journal when she talked about 'secret wayfinding' with H."

I explained my theory about the three points, how the bird-arrow at the river stone already suggested a direction downstream, and how the "3" on Hezekiah's obelisk and at the Guardian Oak might signify something more than just their presence. "What if," I said, tracing lines between the dots on my map, "it's a sequence? Or if one clue tells you how to use the information from another?"

Maya listened intently, her earlier skepticism replaced by a thoughtful frown. "So, you think it's not just what the clues are, but how they relate to each other spatially?"

"Exactly," I said, relieved she wasn't laughing. "Three points. Maybe the poem tells us the order. 'The river whispers, the old stone sighs' – that was first. 'Beneath the gaze the elders keep' – the churchyard, second. 'Seek the heart where memories dwell' – the Guardian Oak, third."

"Okay," she said slowly. "So, what now? The river stone pointed downstream. The churchyard gave us the number three on Hezekiah's obelisk, near Eleanora. The Oak gave us another three."

"The '3' on the obelisk," I mused, "it faced Eleanora's grave. What if it's not just on the obelisk, but means something from Eleanora's grave, towards the obelisk, maybe three paces, or three markers over?" Sam's innocent comment about sealed crypts and old church diaries being at the Historical Society also played in my mind. Old Grace Churchyard felt central to this.

Maya's eyes lit up. "The Harrison family plot at Old Grace is huge. And there are a lot of old, unmarked graves around there too, from before they kept perfect records. What if Eleanora didn't want her secret buried with her, but near her, in a place only H. would know how to find using their system?"

It felt right. The churchyard was where the "elders kept gaze," it was where Eleanora rested, and it was where one of the "3s" was located.

The next Saturday – after a week of me being a model of reluctant compliance for Mrs. Albright and Aunt Sarah, hyper-aware of Henderson's virtual shadow – Maya and I headed back to Old Grace Churchyard. This time, we went with a clearer purpose. We brought my sketchbook, a small trowel Maya had swiped from the garden shed ("Just in case," she'd said with a determined glint in her eye), and a tape measure Uncle Mark kept in the garage.

We started at Eleanora's grave. The simple stone, with its carved lily, felt both sad and expectant. Then we faced Hezekiah Harrison's imposing obelisk.

"Okay," I said, pulling out my sketch of the obelisk with the tiny number "3" carved into the ivy flourish. "The three was on the side facing her. What if it means three... something... in that direction?"

We measured three paces from Eleanora's headstone directly towards the obelisk. It landed us in an empty patch of ground, slightly depressed, covered in old leaves. Nothing.

"Maybe it's not paces," Maya said, tapping her chin. "Look at the obelisk. It's huge. What if it's about the third decorative element from the bottom on that side? Or the third name listed, if there are multiple Harrisons on it?"

We examined the obelisk minutely. The ivy flourish with the "3" was about waist-high. Counting decorative bands from the bottom, the third one was just above it. We scanned it. Nothing. Hezekiah's name was prominent, but there wasn't a clear "third name" in a sequence that made sense.

Disappointment started to creep in. My brilliant theory was falling flat.

"Wait," Maya said, her eyes fixed on the ground around the base of the obelisk, particularly on the side where the "3" was carved. "The ground here... it's different. Look how the grass grows right up to the base on the other sides, but here, there are these... flat stones, almost like paving, mostly buried."

She was right. Partially hidden by overgrown grass and dirt were several flat, irregular stones forming a rough, narrow pathway or edging along that one side of Hezekiah's monument.

"Okay," I said, the new idea taking shape. "The number three. What if it's the third paving stone along this hidden path, starting from the front corner of the obelisk?"

We counted. One... two... three. The third stone was slightly larger than the others, and it looked a tiny bit looser, one edge slightly raised as if something had shifted beneath it over time.

My heart hammered against my ribs. Maya looked at me, her eyes wide.

"No way," she breathed.

I knelt down, my fingers probing the edges of the stone. It definitely felt less secure than its neighbors. I slipped the edge of the trowel into the crack and pried gently. With a grating sound of stone against dirt and root, it shifted. I pried again, harder this time.

The stone wasn't just a paver. It was a lid.

Beneath it, not a deep crypt, but a small, brick-lined cavity, about a foot square and a couple of feet deep. And nestled inside, protected from the worst of the damp by the surprisingly well-fitted stone, was another wooden box.

It was older, more weathered than the one I'd found in Mrs. Albright's closet, but it was unmistakably a box. Carefully, reverently, I reached down and lifted it out. It was heavy for its size, bound with what looked like tarnished brass bands. There was no lock, but the lid was snug.

This had to be it. Eleanora's personal time capsule. The truth she'd concealed from prying eyes.

Maya and I just stared at it, then at each other, the silence of the ancient churchyard pressing in around us, thick with unspoken history and the weight of imminent discovery.

CHAPTER 21

— · —

ELEANORA'S TRUTH

T he air in Old Grace Churchyard seemed to crackle with a sudden, intense energy. The silence was no longer just the quiet of a forgotten place; it was the silence of held breath, of a story paused for over a century, waiting for its next line. Maya and I knelt beside the dislodged stone, the weathered wooden box sitting on the damp earth between us. It was surprisingly heavy, bound with tarnished brass that glinted dully in the filtered sunlight.

"Are you going to open it?" Maya whispered, her usual composure tinged with an awe I felt mirrored in my own chest.

I nodded, my throat tight. This was it. The culmination of weeks of secret searching, of piecing together Eleanora's cryptic clues. My fingers fumbled slightly as I found the simple, unadorned clasp on the front of the box. It was stiff, resistant, as if reluctant to give up its long-held secrets. With a final, determined push, it gave way with a dry click.

Slowly, almost reverently, I lifted the lid.

The scent that wafted out was of aged paper, dried flowers, and something else – a faint, almost imperceptible perfume, like roses pressed between the pages of an old book. Inside, nestled on what looked like faded, once-blue silk, lay a collection of items, each one radiating an aura of intense personal significance.

There was a bundle of letters, tied with a similar faded blue ribbon to the one that had bound the poem. More of Eleanora's spidery script covered the envelopes, but these were addressed not to a nameless "Journal," but to "My Dearest Henry." And beneath them, another set of letters, the handwriting stronger, more masculine, addressed to "My Eleanora."

Henry. So that was H.

Beside the letters lay a small, exquisitely carved wooden bird – a sparrow, perhaps, its wings poised for flight. It was smooth and dark, clearly made with loving care. Tucked next to it was a single, perfectly preserved pressed flower, a deep crimson verbena, its color still surprisingly vibrant against a square of yellowed card. And finally, lying on top of it all, was a small, leather-bound sketchbook, much thinner than mine, its pages filled with delicate, incredibly detailed pencil drawings.

With trembling hands, I picked up the sketchbook first. Maya leaned closer, her breath catching as I opened it. The pages were filled with portraits. There were several of Eleanora, capturing her with an almost startling intimacy – laughing, pensive, her eyes full of the dreams she'd written about. They were beautiful, infused with a tenderness that made my own chest ache. Then, there were sketches of places – the Guardian Oak, its branches rendered with loving detail; the river bend where the old stone lay; even a quick, evocative sketch of what looked like the interior of a simple craftsman's workshop. And on the last page, a self-portrait of the artist – the young man from the locket. Henry. Beneath it, in small, neat letters, was his full name: Henry Ashton.

"He was an artist," Maya breathed, her voice full of wonder. "He drew these."

I picked up one of Eleanora's letters to Henry, my fingers carefully unfolding the brittle paper. Her words, full of youthful passion and a fierce, protective love, spilled out:

"My Dearest Henry," it began. "Father grows more suspicious with each passing day. His pronouncements against your 'unsuitability' echo in every room of this house. He sees only your lack of fortune, your 'common' trade as a woodcarver and artist, and refuses to acknowledge the richness of your spirit, the beauty you create with your hands and see in the world. He cannot understand that your heart is the truest fortune I could ever desire..."

Another letter detailed their secret meetings, the small gifts exchanged (the carved bird, the pressed flower), their shared dreams of a future where they could be together without judgment, without the heavy weight of her family's disapproval. It painted a vivid picture of a love that was pure and deep, but also fraught with the peril of discovery in a society bound by rigid class distinctions. Hezekiah Harrison, the "Esteemed Founder," would never have accepted a penniless artist for his daughter.

The final item in the box was a single, sealed envelope, addressed in Eleanora's hand to simply: "To a Future Sympathetic Heart."

This was it. Her message in a bottle.

My fingers were surprisingly steady as I broke the wax seal, which bore the faint impression of her lily symbol. Inside, a single sheet of parchment.

"If you are reading this," it began, "then more than a century has likely passed, and the petty tyrannies of my time will have faded to dust. I am Eleanora Mayhew Harrison, and I loved Henry Ashton with all my soul. My father, a man of great standing but little understanding of the human heart, forbade our union. He threatened to disinherit me, to send Henry away, to ruin his reputation and his livelihood. Henry, bless his noble spirit, would have faced it all for me, but I could not bear to see him suffer on my account.

I have been unwell these past months. The doctors whisper of consumption, of a decline they cannot halt. My time, I fear, is short. I cannot bear the thought that our love, so true and bright, will be forgotten, or worse, misremembered as a girlish folly or a stain upon my family's name. Henry is a good man, a man of honor and talent, worthy of far more than this world, or my father, would grant him.

This box contains the small tokens of our affection, the truth of our hearts. I bury it here, at the third stone by my father's monument – a small act of defiance, a secret kept close even in the shadow of his disapproval. It is my hope that someday, someone will find this and understand. Understand that love, in its purest form, transcends station and fortune, and that a life, however short, lived with such love, is a life truly lived.

Remember us. Eleanora M.H., September 1890."

A profound silence settled over us as I finished reading. The story was heartbreakingly simple, yet powerful. A forbidden love, a disapproving father, a young life cut short, and a desperate, enduring wish to be remembered truthfully.

The poignancy of it all, the sheer weight of Eleanora's hope entrusted to this fragile collection of memories, resonated deep within me. I thought of my own mother, of the secrets and misunderstood intentions that had fractured my own family. I thought of the "delinquent" label I carried, the judgment I faced, the way people rarely looked beyond the surface. Eleanora, too, had lived under the weight of others' expectations and disapproval, her true self and her true love hidden away.

Her story wasn't about a grand, scandalous secret that would rock the town. It was smaller, more personal, and infinitely more human. It was about the quiet courage of love in the face of opposition, and the enduring desire for one's truth to be known.

Maya wiped a tear from her eye with the back of her hand. "Wow," she whispered. "She just wanted people to know they were real. That he was a good person."

I nodded, unable to speak for a moment. Eleanora's plea, reaching out across more than a hundred years, had found its sympathetic hearts. And strangely, in uncovering her truth, I felt a tiny, almost imperceptible shift within myself. The world suddenly felt a little less about harsh judgments and a little more about the hidden, vulnerable stories that everyone carries.

CHAPTER 22

— · —

THE RECKONING

The weight of Eleanora's small, weathered box seemed to grow heavier in my hands as Maya and I walked back from Old Grace Churchyard. The afternoon sun, which had felt warm and promising on our way there, now seemed to cast long, contemplative shadows. We'd found Eleanora's truth, but now what? It wasn't a treasure map leading to gold, or a scandalous secret that would bring down a dynasty. It was something far more delicate: a young woman's dying wish to have her love story remembered honestly.

"So," Maya said, breaking the silence as we neared the edge of town, "what are we going to do with it? We can't just... put it back, can we?"

I shook my head. Eleanora had wanted her story found by a "sympathetic heart." Stuffing it back into a hole in the ground felt like a betrayal of that century-old hope. "No. She wanted to be remembered. Her and Henry."

"So, do we, like, announce it to the town crier?" Maya attempted a small joke, but her voice was still subdued. "Call the Havenwood Herald? 'Local Teens Uncover Tragic Love Story'?"

A grim smile touched my lips. "Yeah, probably not. This isn't... sensational. It's just... true." I thought of Mrs. Albright's warning about digging carelessly and unsettling old foundations. But this truth didn't feel like it would cause a collapse; it felt more like it might mend something, fill in a missing piece.

"Mrs. Albright," I said finally. "We should show it to her."

Maya looked surprised. "Really? After she practically warned you off digging into old secrets?"

"Yeah," I said, though a knot of apprehension tightened in my stomach. "She's the keeper of Havenwood's history. If anyone knows what to do with this, how to handle it respectfully, it's her. And Eleanora's journal, the first one, came from the Historical Society's donations anyway, even if it was hidden. This all sort of belongs in her domain." It was a risk. Mrs. Albright could confiscate it, bury it again in some archive, or worse, tell Aunt Sarah I'd been snooping where I shouldn't. But it also felt like the right first step.

The next morning, my community service hours felt different. Instead of just going through the motions, I had a purpose. The wooden box, wrapped carefully in an old t-shirt, was heavy in my backpack. Maya had insisted on coming with me, for moral support, she said, though I suspected she was just as invested in seeing Mrs. Albright's reaction as I was.

We found Mrs. Albright in her usual spot, poring over a fragile, yellowed map. She looked up as we approached, her sharp eyes taking in both of us, then the slightly bulging shape of my backpack.

"Mr. Carter. Miss Miller. An unexpected joint visit," she remarked, her tone neutral.

I took a deep breath. "Mrs. Albright," I began, "we found something. Something I think you need to see. It's... it's about Eleanora Mayhew Harrison."

Her expression didn't change, but I saw a flicker of something in her eyes – interest? Recognition? She simply gestured to the large oak table in the center of the room. "Then perhaps you should show me."

Carefully, I unwrapped the old wooden box and placed it on the table. Then, I laid out the contents: Eleanora's letters to Henry, his to her, his sketchbook with the portraits, the carved bird, the pressed flower, and finally, Eleanora's last letter, addressed "To a Future Sympathetic Heart."

Maya and I stood in silence as Mrs. Albright, with surprising gentleness, picked up each item. She read Eleanora's final letter first, her lips moving almost imperceptibly. Her face, usually a mask of stern composure, seemed to soften. She examined Henry's sketches with a keen eye, lingered over the miniature portrait of him in the locket I also produced, and then slowly, methodically, began to read through the letters.

It took a long time. Maya and I exchanged nervous glances. Finally, Mrs. Albright looked up, her gaze resting on me, then Maya.

"Remarkable," she said, her voice quiet, almost a whisper. "Truly remarkable. Henry Ashton... I've seen his name in passing, in old town ledgers. A carpenter's apprentice, later listed as a carver and itinerant artist. Always on the fringes. Never connected with the Harrisons, of course." She shook her head slowly. "Hezekiah Harrison was a formidable man. Proud. Unyielding. This... this would have been unthinkable to him."

She paused, looking at the collection again. "Eleanora was right to want this remembered. It's a testament to a love that defied the conventions of her time. A very human story amidst the official histories."

"So... what happens now?" I asked, my voice barely above a whisper.

"Now," Mrs. Albright said, a new decisiveness in her tone, "we do right by Eleanora. And by Henry."

Over the next few weeks, with Mrs. Albright's careful guidance, Eleanora's story began to quietly unfold, not as a scandal, but as a poignant piece of Havenwood's rich tapestry. Mrs. Albright, it turned out, was a distant relative of another old Havenwood family that had known the Harrisons. She contacted the few remaining Harrison descendants, scattered across the country, sharing Eleanora's story with sensitivity and respect.

There was no big newspaper exposé. Instead, for the upcoming Founder's Day exhibit, Mrs. Albright decided to create a small, special display dedicated to Eleanora and Henry. It featured facsimiles of some of the letters, prints of

Henry's sketches (including his self-portrait and his draw-ings of Eleanora), the carved bird, and a carefully worded narrative explaining their story and Eleanora's wish. The original items, she explained, would be preserved in the Historical Society's secure archives.

The exhibit, when it opened, did cause a stir, but it was mostly a quiet one. People lingered by the display, reading the letters, their expressions touched, thoughtful. Some older residents remembered hearing vague family whis-pers about a "tragic Harrison girl" from long ago. Others, descendants of families who had also perhaps bristled under Hezekiah Harrison's stern influence, found a certain satisfaction in this more human, vulnerable portrayal of his era.

No one made a hero out of me. I was still the "troubled kid from the city." But as I stood in the corner of the exhibit hall during the Founder's Day reception, watching people engage with Eleanora's truth, I felt an unfamiliar sense of... not pride, exactly, but quiet accomplishment. I hadn't set out to change anything, just to solve a puzzle. But in bring-ing Eleanora's hidden story to light, respectfully, something had shifted. It was like a small, almost invisible crack had appeared in the town's perfectly preserved facade, letting in a little more honesty, a little more understanding of the complex, often messy, human hearts that had shaped its past.

And maybe, just maybe, it was helping to do the same for mine.

Chapter 23

Facing the Judge, Facing Himself

The Founder's Day exhibit, with its quiet corner dedicated to Eleanora and Henry, marked a kind of turning point in Havenwood, at least for me. It wasn't a dramatic shift, just a subtle easing of the tension I always felt coiled in my chest. People didn't suddenly start treating me like a hero – I was still Liam Carter, the kid who'd smashed windows and been shipped off to avoid juvie. But some of the curious stares I received felt less judgmental now, more... thoughtful. Maybe they saw that even a "delinquent" could stumble upon something meaningful. Or maybe it was just my imagination.

The real test, however, wasn't the opinion of Havenwood's residents. It was the impending video conference with Judge Ramirez, scheduled for the week after Founder's Day. Mr. Henderson, my probation officer, would be facilitating, and both Dad and Aunt Sarah would be present, physically or virtually. This was it – the moment to see if my summer of forced relocation and accidental historical detective work had made any difference in the eyes of the law.

The days leading up to it were a blur of anxiety. I re-played Mr. Henderson's earlier criticisms in my head: not seeing much proactive engagement... demonstrable re-morse... significant turnaround. Had I shown any of that? My involvement with Eleanora's story hadn't been about trying to impress a judge; it had been a personal obsession, a secret I'd pursued for my own reasons.

The conference took place in Uncle Mark's small home office. The laptop was set up on his desk, and I sat there awkwardly, Aunt Sarah beside me offering a small, reas-suring smile that didn't quite reach her worried eyes. Dad's face appeared on screen, looking tired but also, I thought, a little less strained than before. Then Mr. Henderson, all professional composure. And finally, Judge Ramirez, her expression as stern and unreadable as it had been in the courtroom.

Mr. Henderson started, summarizing my "adherence to the basic terms" of my placement – community service hours completed (thanks to Mrs. Albright's endless boxes), online coursework maintained, curfews met. It sounded like the bare minimum, just as he'd said before. My stomach sank.

Then he paused. "However," he continued, a new note in his voice, "there have been some... notable developments. Mrs. Elspeth Albright, curator of the Havenwood Historical Society, submitted an unsolicited letter regarding Liam's contributions."

My head snapped up. Mrs. Albright?

Mr. Henderson read from the letter. It was concise, formal, and surprisingly... positive. She detailed my initial reluctance, yes, but then went on to describe my "unexpected diligence" in the archives, my "keen observational skills," and, to my utter astonishment, my "instrumental role in uncovering and respectfully bringing to light a significant and poignant piece of Havenwood's local history, the story of Eleanora Mayhew Harrison and Henry Ashton." She even mentioned the care with which Maya and I had handled the delicate artifacts. She concluded by saying that while my initial attitude had been "challenging," my recent focus and the positive outcome of my "independent research" suggested a "capacity for thoughtful engagement and responsibility not previously apparent."

I was stunned. Mrs. Albright, Elspeth the Eternal, had actually gone to bat for me.

Aunt Sarah then spoke, her voice clear and steady. She didn't paint me as a saint. She acknowledged the difficulties, my withdrawn nature, my initial resentment. But she also spoke of the small changes she'd seen – my willingness, however reluctant, to help Maya with the Eleanora mystery, the way I'd seemed to connect with that story, the flicker of something other than anger in my eyes on occasion. She spoke of the cookies she'd left me that night, and how it felt like a tiny step, not a solution, but a beginning.

Dad added a few words, his voice thick with emotion, about how he hoped this summer had given me a chance to breathe, to think, to find a different path.

Finally, Judge Ramirez looked at me, her gaze still intense. "Liam Carter," she said. "This is... more than I expected. Mrs. Albright is not known for her effusive praise." A ghost of a smile touched her lips. "It seems you've been doing more than just 'serving time' in Havenwood. Tell me, what has this experience, particularly this discovery of Eleanora Harrison's story, meant to you?"

The question caught me off guard. I wasn't prepared for introspection, just for judgment. I fumbled for words. "I... I don't know. It was just... a puzzle at first. Something to do." I thought of Eleanora's letters, H.'s portrait, their hidden love. "But then... it started to feel real. Her story, it was... sad. But she was strong, too, trying to make sure her truth wasn't lost. She was judged by her father, misunderstood. And H... he was a good guy, but nobody saw it because he didn't fit their idea of who he should be."

I paused, the connection suddenly clear in my own mind. "I guess... I guess I know a little bit about what that feels like. To be seen as one thing, when there's more going on underneath that nobody bothers to look for." I thought of the rage that had led to the vandalism, the years of pain over my mother's abandonment that had fueled it. It wasn't an excuse, not even close. But it was... context. A hidden story.

"Finding Eleanora's box," I finished, my voice quiet, "it felt like I was helping someone else's truth get out. And maybe... maybe that matters."

The courtroom video feed was silent for a long moment. Judge Ramirez studied me, her expression unreadable. Then, she nodded slowly.

"Mr. Carter," she said, "your actions that led you to my courtroom were serious. They spoke of anger, disrespect, and a lack of concern for consequences. What I've heard today, however, and what I see in your attempt to articulate your experience, suggests that perhaps Havenwood has offered you more than just an escape from detention. It has offered you a chance for reflection, and perhaps, the beginnings of empathy – for others, and maybe even for yourself."

She took a breath. "Given the reports from Mrs. Albright and your aunt, and your own... surprisingly insightful comments, the court is willing to amend your disposition. The remainder of your sentence will be converted to supervised probation, to be completed in your father's care back in the city. This is contingent on continued counseling and full adherence to the terms of your probation. No more chances, Liam. This is it."

Relief washed over me, so potent it left me lightheaded. No juvie. I was going home. Probation wasn't freedom, not by a long shot, but it was a world away from where I could have been.

"Thank you, Your Honor," I managed, my voice hoarse.

"Don't thank me, Mr. Carter," she said, her expression softening almost imperceptibly. "Thank your aunt and uncle for their willingness to open their home. Thank Mrs. Albright for seeing something in you worth writing about. And perhaps, thank Eleanora Harrison for reminding you that everyone has a story, and that some are worth uncovering."

The call ended. I sat there, stunned, as Aunt Sarah squeezed my arm, her eyes shining with tears. Dad's relieved face on the screen was a balm to my own raw nerves.

I wasn't "fixed." I wasn't suddenly a new person. But something had shifted. In facing Eleanora's past, in helping her truth to surface, I had, in some small, unexpected way, begun to face myself. And for the first time in a very long time, the path ahead didn't look entirely like a dead end.

CHAPTER 24

— · —

SEEDS OF CHANGE

The days following the video conference with Judge Ramirez felt strangely light. The oppressive weight of a potential juvie sentence was gone, replaced by the slightly less daunting prospect of probation back home. It wasn't freedom, not yet, but it was a reprieve, a chance to breathe. Havenwood, once my prison, now felt more like a temporary harbor, a quiet place where I'd weathered a significant storm.

My last Sunday in Havenwood arrived, bathed in the warm glow of late summer. When Aunt Sarah asked if I'd be joining them for church, there was no pressure in her voice, just a gentle invitation. To my own surprise, a quiet "Yeah, I think I will" came out before I could second-guess it. The memory of my first disastrous Sunday, feeling singled out by Pastor Evans' sermon on the Prodigal Son, still made me cringe. But something was different now. Maybe it was Eleanora's story, the raw honesty of her faith and her struggles. Maybe it was Aunt Sarah's unwavering, quiet grace. Or maybe it was just the slow unclenching of the fist that had been wrapped around my heart for so long.

This time, walking into Havenwood Community Church, I didn't feel like an alien under a microscope. There were still friendly nods and polite smiles, but instead of seeing judgment, I saw... community. People greeting each other, sharing snippets of their lives, a low hum of genuine connection. I didn't slouch in the pew, didn't cross my arms. I just sat, breathing in the scent of old wood and coffee, and for the first time, I simply listened.

Pastor Evans' sermon wasn't about prodigals today. He spoke about finding light in unexpected places, about how even in our deepest valleys or most confusing detours, God's presence could be found, often in the quiet whispers, in the kindness of others, in the courage to face our own truths. He read a passage about hope being an anchor for the soul.

And this time, the words didn't feel like accusations. They didn't feel directed at me. Instead, they settled into a space within me that had felt empty for a very long time. I thought of Eleanora's small, hidden box, a truth waiting patiently in the darkness. I thought of Aunt Sarah's hand on my arm, her unexpected story of her own wavering faith. I thought of the surprising camaraderie with Maya as we hunted for clues. Little glimmers, she'd called them.

During one of the hymns, a simple melody with words about seeking and finding, I didn't sing – that still felt like a bridge too far – but I read the words in the hymnal. "Draw me nearer, nearer, blessed Lord, to the cross where Thou hast died. Draw me nearer, nearer, nearer, blessed Lord, to Thy precious, bleeding side." A strange longing stirred in my chest, an ache that wasn't entirely pain. It was a yearning for... something more. For the peace that seemed to settle on Aunt Sarah's face when she prayed, for the sense of belonging that filled this simple room. For a connection to this God who supposedly offered light in darkness, hope to the lost. For the first time, the thought of getting closer to Him didn't feel like an obligation or a threat, but like a possibility, a tentative, almost fearful desire.

My last few days with Aunt Sarah, Uncle Mark, Maya, and Sam were different after that. The ever-present tension in my shoulders seemed to ease a fraction. I still wasn't Mr. Sunshine, but the constant scowl felt less fixed, less necessary.

One evening, I found Aunt Sarah alone on the porch swing, watching the fireflies begin their nightly dance in the dusky yard. The scent of honeysuckle hung heavy in the air. I hesitated, then walked over and sat on the steps near her.

"So," she said softly, her voice kind, "you'll be heading home soon."

"Yeah," I said. "Next week, Dad's driving down to get me."

We sat in comfortable silence for a few moments.

"Aunt Sarah," I began, the words feeling awkward but necessary. "I... uh... I wanted to say thanks. For... you know. Everything." I gestured vaguely to the house, the town, the general situation. "For not giving up on me, even when I was being a... well, you know."

She smiled, a genuine, warm smile that reached her eyes. "Oh, Liam. We were glad to have you. Truly. It wasn't always easy," she chuckled softly, "but then, family rarely is, is it?"

"That letter from Mrs. Albright helped a lot, I think," I said.

"Elspeth has a keen eye for character," Aunt Sarah said. "She saw you, Liam. Just like Mark and I did." She paused. "This Eleanora you found... it seems she helped you find something too. And your experience in church last Sunday... you seemed more at peace."

I nodded, looking out at the blinking fireflies. "Her story... it was different than I expected. She was judged, but she still held onto what mattered to her." I took a breath. "And church... it felt different too. Pastor Evans' words about hope... I actually listened. I still don't get a lot of it, the God stuff. Especially after Mom leaving, it's hard to... trust in something you can't see, something that's supposed to be good when things go so wrong."

"Faith isn't about having all the answers, Liam," she said gently, her earlier words echoing. "It's a journey, full of questions. Even Jesus's closest followers had doubts. The important thing is the desire to seek, to be open to that Light, even when it's faint." She reached over and briefly squeezed my hand. "That longing you feel, that desire to know... that's a precious thing, Liam. That's where the journey begins."

It wasn't a conversion moment. No choirs sang. But sitting there, I felt that tiny seed of something other than bitterness take root a little deeper. Maybe, just maybe, there were ways of looking at the world, at faith, at people, that I was only just beginning to consider. And maybe, this time, I wouldn't stomp on that seed before it had a chance to grow.

The phone call to Dad later that week was different too. He sounded lighter, more hopeful. We talked about practical things, and then I found myself telling him a little about Eleanora, and even, hesitantly, about how church hadn't been totally awful the last time. He just listened, a warmth in his voice I hadn't heard in a long time.

"Sounds like you're figuring some things out, son," he said.

I even managed a slightly less awkward call with Chloe. She was still stressed, but she listened when I told her, haltingly, that maybe one bad grade wasn't the end of the world, that sometimes things go wrong but you find a way through. Ben just wanted to know if God lived in the fireflies. I told him I wasn't sure, but it was a nice thought.

My last evening in Havenwood, I sat at the desk in my room, my sketchbook open. I flipped through the pages. The early drawings were dark, filled with cages, broken things, shadowed figures. Then came the sketches of Eleanora's clues – more focused, driven by the puzzle.

And then, the newer sketches. There was one of the Guardian Oak, sunlight filtering through its leaves. There was a drawing of the view from my window, not just the confining backyard, but the wide expanse of sky above it, a single star prominent. There was even a quick sketch of the inside of the little church, not the people, but the light coming through the stained-glass window.

The lines felt different. Less angry. More... open. As if, in uncovering Eleanora's hidden connections, and in allowing myself to feel that tiny, tentative stirring of faith, I'd started to see a few new connections of my own, however fragile.

I wasn't leaving Havenwood the same person who had arrived. The anger was still there, a familiar ember, but it didn't burn quite so hot. The cynicism hadn't vanished, but it was now tinged with a reluctant curiosity, a hesitant awareness that not everything, and not everyone, was exactly as it seemed on the surface.

The seeds of change, I realized, had been quietly sown in the still waters of this unexpected town. And I had a feeling they'd continue to grow, long after I'd gone.

Chapter 25

— · —

A New Horizon

The last days of August in Havenwood were draped in a hazy, golden light, the kind that signals the end of one season and the quiet approach of another. My duffel bag, which had felt so heavy with despair when I first arrived, now sat by the door of my bluebird room, packed with clothes that smelled faintly of Aunt Sarah's laundry detergent and a summer I'd never forget. Dad was due to arrive in a few hours. My time in this unexpected harbor was coming to an end.

I wasn't the same kid who'd been dragged here under a court order, simmering with rage and resentment. That angry, defensive shell hadn't shattered completely – it was probably a part of me I'd always carry, a scar from old wounds. But it was thinner now, more porous, allowing glimpses of something else to seep through. Hope, maybe. Or at least the possibility of it.

My probation back in the city wouldn't be easy. There would be check-ins with a new officer, mandatory counseling sessions that would probably dredge up all the stuff I still wasn't ready to talk about concerning Mom, and the constant awareness that I was one screw-up away from bigger trouble. But the thought of it no longer filled me with pure dread. It felt... manageable. A path to walk, not a dead end.

Aunt Sarah found me on the porch swing, the same spot where we'd had our quiet talk. She handed me a small, lumpy package wrapped in brown paper and string. "A little something to remember us by," she said, her smile a bit watery.

Inside was a new sketchbook, much nicer than my battered old one, and a set of artist-grade drawing pencils. Tucked within the pages was a small, smooth stone from the banks of the Stillwater River, and a pressed verbena flower, a deep crimson, just like the one Eleanora had treasured from Henry.

"I... Aunt Sarah, this is..." I was speechless.

"Every artist needs good tools," she said softly. "And every journey needs a few touchstones to remind you where you've been, and what you've learned." She sat beside me. "You know, Liam, this house is going to feel awfully quiet without you brooding in the corners." There was a teasing lilt in her voice, but her eyes were full of genuine affection.

"Yeah, well, don't get too used to the peace and quiet," I managed, a small smile tugging at my own lips. "Maybe I'll actually call once in a while."

"We'd like that very much," Uncle Mark said, joining us on the porch, Sam and Maya trailing behind him.

Sam, bless his unfiltered heart, immediately launched into a detailed explanation of why I should take him back to the city to fight "real bad guys." Maya, more reserved, just gave me a small, almost shy smile. "Don't go smashing any more windows, city boy," she said, but there was no malice in it, only a kind of teasing affection that made my chest feel surprisingly warm.

"Wouldn't dream of it," I said. We'd even managed a few more awkward conversations since our Guardian Oak adventure, a tentative friendship forming over shared eye-rolls at Sam's antics and a grudging mutual respect.

Later, as Dad's familiar, beat-up sedan pulled into the driveway, I took one last look around. At the neat white house with its green shutters, at the wide porch, at the faces of this family who had taken in a broken, angry kid and shown him nothing but stubborn kindness.

The goodbyes were heartfelt but not overly dramatic. Aunt Sarah hugged me tight, whispering, "Remember those glimmers, Liam. And know you're always welcome here." Uncle Mark clapped me on the shoulder, a rare smile on his face. "You did good, son. Keep heading in the right direction."

As Dad and I drove away from Havenwood, the town square receding in the rearview mirror, I didn't feel the desperate urge to escape that I'd anticipated. Instead, there was a quiet sort of ache, a recognition that I was leaving behind something important, something that had changed me in ways I was still only beginning to understand.

"So," Dad said, glancing over at me, "ready to be home?"

"Yeah," I said. And for the first time in what felt like forever, it didn't feel like a lie. Home was still complicated. My relationship with Chloe and Ben needed work. My own internal landscape was still full of shadows. But it wasn't a battlefield anymore. Maybe, just maybe, it could be a place to start rebuilding.

I thought of Eleanora and Henry, their story now a small, quiet part of Havenwood's official history, their love remembered. Their truth had come out, not in a blaze of glory, but in a gentle unfolding. Maybe my own truth, my own path, would unfold in a similar way – not with sudden, dramatic transformations, but with small steps, quiet realizations, and the courage to keep seeking the light, however faint it sometimes seemed.

My new sketchbook lay on the seat beside me. I picked it up, feeling the quality of the paper, the smooth wood of the pencils. I didn't know what I would draw first. Maybe just the horizon line, stretching out towards an unknown future. A future that, thanks to a summer of Stillwater secrets and unexpected grace, finally felt like it might hold some promise after all.

—·—

ABOUT THE AUTHOR

I've spent over four decades watching and participating in the digital revolution. From my first encounters with computer programming in high school during the late 1970s to navigating today's complex cyber landscape, technology has been a constant companion in my journey. While serving in the U.S. Army during Desert Storm, I witnessed firsthand how rapidly technology could evolve and transform our capabilities.

Now, as I navigate my senior years, I find myself in a unique position – someone who understands both the tremendous potential and the growing challenges of our digital age. This book represents not just my knowledge, but our shared experience as we continue to adapt and learn in this ever-changing digital world.

Through her writing, Rene' aims to illuminate the positive aspects of life's journey, drawing from her varied experiences to create stories that resonate with readers of all backgrounds.

Readers can discover more about Rene's work at www.books-by-rene.store

www.ingramcontent.com/pod-product-compliance
Lightning Source LLC
Chambersburg PA
CBHW020231120726
47903CB00008B/2625